This book belongs to

....

CLASSIC TREASURY

BEDTIME STORIES

Compiled by Tig Thomas

Miles Kelly

First published in 2014 by Miles Kelly Publishing Ltd
Harding's Barn, Bardfield End Green, Thaxted, Essex, CM6 3PX, UK

Copyright © Miles Kelly Publishing Ltd 2014

Some of this material was first published in 2009 by
Miles Kelly Publishing Ltd as part of *50 Bedtime Stories*

2 4 6 8 10 9 7 5 3 1

Publishing Director *Belinda Gallagher*
Creative Director *Jo Cowan*
Editorial Director *Rosie Neave*
Senior Editors *Sarah Parkin, Claire Philip*
Designers *Rob Hale, Joe Jones*
Production Manager *Elizabeth Collins*
Reprographics *Stephan Davis, Jennifer Cozens, Thom Allaway*

ISBN 978-1-78209-584-2

Printed in China

British Library Cataloguing-in-Publication Data
A catalogue record for this book is available from the British Library

ACKNOWLEDGEMENTS
The publishers would like to thank the following artists
who have contributed to this book:
Cover
Central image: Natalia Moore
Other elements: Alice Brisland at The Bright Agency, LenLis/Shutterstock.com,
kusuriuri/Shutterstock.com, Lana L/Shutterstock.com, Markovka/Shutterstock.com
Inside pages
Advocate Art: Andy Catling
Beehive Illustration: Rupert Van Wyk
The Bright Agency: Mark Beech, Peter Cottrill, Evelyne Duverne,
Masumi Furukawa, Tom Sperling

Made with paper from a sustainable forest

www.mileskelly.net
info@mileskelly.net

CONTENTS

BOLD LADS AND BRAVE GIRLS

STRANGE AND MAGICAL TALES

ALONG THE ROAD

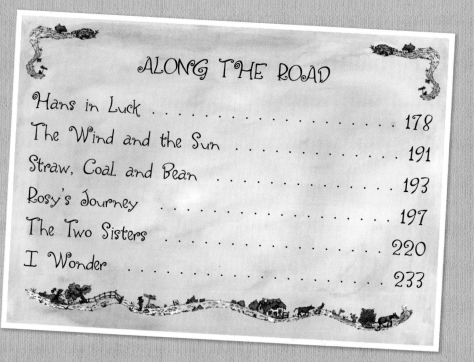

WHAT NONSENSE!

BIRDS, BEASTS AND DRAGONS

ABOUT THE AUTHORS

Learn more about some of the famous authors behind these much-loved stories.

Louisa May Alcott
1832–1888

Little Women is Alcott's most famous book. She began it in the hope it might pay off some of her family's debts. In it, she told stories from her own childhood with her sisters May, Elizabeth and Anna. The book was an enormous success and Alcott became both wealthy and an unwilling celebrity.

Hans Christian Andersen
1805–1875

Born in Denmark, Andersen was apprenticed to a weaver and a tailor, before working as an actor and singer in Copenhagen. While in the theatre he wrote poetry and stories, and became famous worldwide for children's tales. These have been translated into over 150 languages, and have inspired movies, plays and ballets.

L Frank Baum
1856–1919

Lyman Frank Baum was born in New York, USA. He hated his first name and preferred to be called Frank. Baum's greatest success was *The Wonderful Wizard of Oz*. He went on to write 13 books about the magical land of Oz, and many other short stories, poems and scripts.

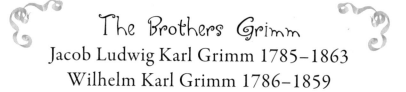

The Brothers Grimm
Jacob Ludwig Karl Grimm 1785–1863
Wilhelm Karl Grimm 1786–1859

Jacob and Wilhelm Grimm were born near Frankfurt, Germany. They read law at university, but were inspired to study how spoken language changes over time. This led them to collect many popular oral European folk tales and set them down on paper. Jacob did most of the research while Wilhelm did more of the writing. The brothers became librarians and also worked on compiling language books and a dictionary.

About the Authors

Joseph Jacobs
1854–1916

Born in Australia, Jacobs studied in England and Germany as a young man, researching Jewish history. Eventually he settled in America, and went on to edit five collections of fairy tales.

Rudyard Kipling
1865–1936

Kipling was born in India, but lived in England from the age of five. He became one of Britain's best-loved poets and children's writers for works including *Just So Stories* and *The Jungle Book*.

Andrew Lang
1844–1912

Scotsman Lang studied at St Andrew's University in Fife and Balliol College, Oxford. He researched folklore, mythology and religion, and wrote poetry and novels. Lang adapted 12 books of folk and fairy tales for children.

Yei Theodora Ozaki
?–1933

Ozaki was born into nobility, and married Yukio Ozaki, the Mayor of Tokyo, who was influential in international politics. Her lifelong passion was collecting and retelling ancient Japanese folk tales.

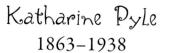

Katharine Pyle
1863–1938

Born into a warm and creative Quaker household, Pyle, like her brother Howard, worked all her life as a writer and illustrator.

Flora Annie Steel
1847–1929

Spending 22 years living in India, Steel involved herself in all sorts of projects, which included acting as a school inspector and collecting local folklore.

ABOUT THE ARTISTS

Mark Beech was inspired by the illustrations of Edward Lear and Lewis Caroll, and loved illustrating their stories himself. He has now worked in most areas of illustration, but loves children's publishing best of all.

The Ogre's Bride • The Haughty Princess • Carrie's Three Wishes
The Three Sillies • The Two Frogs

Andy Catling is based in Hampshire, in the UK. He likes to work with watercolour, gouache and ink, and is the proud owner of a very messy work table, an excessive number of brushes and one very old mechanical pencil.

Empty Bottles • Rosy's Journey • My Lord Bag of Rice
Page decoration throughout

Peter Cottrill is inspired by humour and a sense of the absurd. He enjoys creating stories and scenarios. As well as illustrating books, Peter does some teaching and practises Shiatsu.

The Clever Apprentice • The Wise Girl • The Wind and the Sun
I Wonder • Nasreddin Hodja and the Smell of Soup
Nasreddin Hodja and the Pot • How the Camel got his Hump

Evelyne Duverne is a freelance painter-illustrator. She works with acrylics on paper, canvas and cardboard. Evelyne especially likes to draw characters, getting her inspiration from the legends and tales she read as a child.

Cap o' Rushes • Tattercoats • The Golden Snuff Box • The Husband
of the Rat's Daughter • The Two Sisters • Tikki Tikki Tembo

About the Artists

Masumi Furukawa lives in Tokyo, Japan. She illustrates and writes children's books. Masumi has worked on many books with different publishers all over the world.

The Fish and the Ring • Hans in Luck • Straw, Coal and Bean
The Sagacious Monkey and the Boar • Why the Swallow's Tail is Forked

Natalia Moore is a qualified art teacher and freelance illustrator. She works with mixed media and puts in the finishing touches digitally. Natalia likes to draw from real-life and is never without her sketchbook.

Cover

Tom Sperling pursued his interest in illustration by studying at The Art Student's League of New York. He has twice been awarded the Paul Revere Award for Graphic Excellence, and won the Small Press Book Award for Best Illustrated Young Adult Book.

The Broad Man, the Tall Man, and the Man with Eyes of Flame
The Three Aunts • The Seven Little Kids

Rupert Van Wyk has been drawing from a very young age. His work has been published in the UK, Italy, United States and South Korea. Rupert lives and works between Ravenna, Italy and London, UK.

The Four Clever Brothers • The Swineherd • The Husband who was to
Mind the House • Sir Gammer Vans • Lazy Jack • The Girl who
Owned a Bear • How the Rhinoceros got his Skin

BOLD LADS AND BRAVE GIRLS

The Clever Apprentice 58

The Wise Girl 62

The Ogre's Bride 76

The Fish
and the Ring

By Flora Annie Steel

*O*nce upon a time there lived a baron who was
a great magician, and could tell by his arts
and charms absolutely everything that was going to
happen at any time.

Now this great lord had a little son born to him
as heir to all his castles and lands. So, when the little
lad was about four years old, wishing to know what
his fortune would be, the baron looked in his Book

of Fate to see what it foretold.

And, lo and behold! It was written that this much-loved, much-prized heir to all the great lands and castles was to marry a low-born maiden. The baron was dismayed – he wanted his son to marry a royal. So he set to work by more arts and charms to discover if this maiden were already born, and if so, where she lived.

And he found out that she had just been born in a very poor house, where the poor parents already had five children.

So he called for his horse and rode far away, until he came to the poor man's house, and there he found the poor man sitting at his doorstep very sad and doleful.

"What is the matter, my friend?" asked he, and the poor man replied:

"May it please your honour, a little lass has just been born to our house, and we have five children already, and where the bread is to come from to fill the sixth mouth, we know not."

"If that be all your trouble," said the baron readily, "maybe I can help you. So don't be downhearted. I am just looking for such a little lass to be a companion to my son, so, if you will, I will give you ten crowns for her."

Well! The man sat and thought for a while. He didn't want to part with his baby, but he needed the money badly. So, he stood up and shook the baron's hand, glad that his daughter was to go to a good home, or so he thought.

Therefore he brought out the child then and there, and the baron, wrapping the babe in his cloak, took her and rode away. But as soon as he got to the river he flung the little thing into the swollen stream, and said to himself as he galloped back to his castle:

"There goes Fate!"

But, you see, he was just mistaken. For the little lass didn't sink. The stream was very swift, and her long clothes kept her up till she caught in a snag just opposite a fisherman, who was mending his nets.

Now the fisherman and his wife had no children, and they were just longing for a baby, so when the good man saw the little lass he was overcome with joy, and took her home to his wife, who received her with open arms. And there she grew up, the apple of their eyes, into the most beautiful maiden that ever was seen.

Now, when she was about fifteen years of age, it so happened that the baron and his friends went hunting along the banks of the river and stopped to get a drink of water at the fisherman's hut. And who should bring the water out but, as they thought, the fisherman's daughter.

They noticed her beauty, and one of them said to the baron, "She should marry well, read us her fate, since you are so learned in the art."

The baron, scarce looking at her, said carelessly, "I could guess her fate! Some wretched yokel. But, to please you, I will cast her horoscope by the stars, so tell me, girl, what day you were born?"

"That I cannot tell, sir," replied the girl, "for I was picked up in the river about fifteen years ago."

Then the baron grew pale, for he guessed at once that she was the little lass he had flung into the stream, and that Fate had been stronger than he was. But he said nothing at the time. Afterwards, however, he thought out a plan, so he rode back and gave the girl a letter.

"See you!" he said. "I will make your fortune. Take this letter to my brother, who needs a good girl, and you will be settled for life."

Now the fisherman and his wife were growing old and needed help, so the girl said she would go, and took the letter. The baron rode back to his castle saying to himself once more:

"There goes Fate!"

For what he had written in the letter was this:

Dear Brother, take the bearer and put her to death immediately.

But once again he was sorely mistaken, since on the way to the town where his brother lived, the girl had to stop the night in a little inn. And it so happened that that very night a gang of thieves broke into the inn, and not content with carrying off all that the innkeeper possessed, they searched the pockets of the guests, and found the letter which the girl carried. And when they read it, they agreed that it was a mean trick and a shame. So their captain sat down and, taking pen and paper, wrote instead:

> Dear Brother, take the bearer and marry her to my son without delay.

Then, after putting the note into an envelope and sealing it up, they gave it to the girl and bade her go on her way. So when she arrived at the brother's castle, though rather surprised, he gave orders for a wedding feast to be prepared. And the baron's son, who was staying with his uncle, seeing the girl's great beauty, was not unwilling, so they were quickly married.

Well! When the news was brought to the baron, he was beside himself, but he was determined not to be outdone by Fate. So he rode quickly to his brother's and pretended to be quite pleased. And then one day, when no one was near, he asked the young bride to come for a walk with him, and when they were close to some cliffs, seized hold of her, and was for throwing her over into the sea. But she begged hard for her life.

"It is not my fault," she said. "I have done nothing. It is Fate. But if you will spare my life I promise that I will fight against Fate also. I will never see you or your son again until you desire it. That will be safer for you, since, see you, the sea may preserve me, as the river did."

Well! The baron agreed to this. So he took off his gold ring from his finger and flung it over the cliffs into the sea and said:

"Never dare to show me your face again till you can show me that ring likewise."

And with that he let her go.

Well! The girl wandered on, and she wandered on, until she came to a nobleman's castle, and there, as they needed a kitchen girl, she took work.

Now, one day, as she was cleaning a big fish, she looked out of the kitchen window, and who should she see driving up to dinner but the baron and his young son, her husband. She was about to run away when she remembered they would not see her in the kitchen, so she went on cleaning the big fish.

And, lo and behold! She saw something shine in its inside. There, sure enough, was the baron's ring! She slipped it on to her thumb, and went on with her work, dressing the fish as nicely as ever she could. Then the girl served it up prettily, with parsley sauce and butter.

Well! When it came to table the guests liked it so well that they asked the host who cooked it. And he called to his servants, "Send up the cook who cooked that fine fish, that she may get her reward."

Well! When the girl heard she was wanted she made herself ready, and with the gold ring on her thumb, went boldly into the dining hall. And all the guests when they saw her were struck dumb by her wonderful beauty. And the young husband started up gladly, but the baron jumped up angrily and looked as if he would kill her.

So, without one word, the girl held up her hand before his face, and the gold ring shone and glittered on it, and she went straight up to the baron, and laid her hand with the ring on it before him on the table.

Then the baron understood that Fate had been too strong for him once again, so he took her by the hand, and, placing her beside him, turned to the guests and said:

"Everyone, this is my son's wife. Let us drink a toast in her honour."

And after dinner he took her and his son home to his castle, where they all lived as happy as could be forever afterwards.

Cap o' Rushes

By Joseph Jacobs

There was once a very rich gentleman, who had three daughters, and he thought he'd see how fond they were of him. So he said to the first, "How much do you love me, my dear?"

"Why," said she, "as I love my life."

"That's good," said he.

So he said to the second, "How much do you love me, my dear?"

"Why," said she, "better than all the world."

"That's good," said he.

So he said to the third, "How much do you love me, my dear?"

"I love you as fresh meat loves salt," said she.

Well, he was angry. "You don't love me at all," said he, "and in my house you stay no more." So he drove her out there and then, and shut the door in her face.

Well, she went away on and on till she came to a fen, and there she gathered a lot of rushes and made them into a kind of cloak with a hood, to cover her from head to foot, and to hide her fine clothes. And then she went on till she came to a great house.

"Do you want a maid?" said she.

"No, we don't," said they.

"I have nowhere to go," said she, "and I ask no wages, and do any sort of work," said she.

"Well," said they, "if you like to wash the pots and scrape the saucepans you may stay."

So she stayed there and washed the pots and scraped the saucepans and did all the dirty work.

Cap o' Rushes

And because she gave no name they called her 'Cap o' Rushes'.

Well, one day there was to be a great dance a little way off, and the servants were allowed to go and look on at the grand people. Cap o' Rushes said she was too tired to go, so she stayed at home.

But as soon as they were gone, she took off her cap o' rushes and cleaned herself, and went to the dance. There was no one at the dance so finely dressed as she.

Well, who should be there but her master's son, and what should he do but fall in love with her the minute he set eyes on her. He wouldn't dance with anyone else.

But before the dance was done, Cap o' Rushes slipped off, and away she went home. When the other maids came back, she was pretending to be asleep with her cap o' rushes on.

Well, next morning they said to her, "You did miss a sight, Cap o' Rushes!"

"What was that?" said she.

"Why, the beautifullest lady you ever saw was there. She dressed right gay and grand. The young master, he never took his eyes off her and they danced all night long."

"Well, I should have liked to have seen her," said Cap o' Rushes.

"Well, there's to be another dance this evening, and perhaps she'll be there."

But, come the evening, Cap o' Rushes said she was too tired to go with them. However, when they were gone, she took off her cap o' rushes and cleaned herself, and away she went to the dance, like the night before.

The master's son had been hoping to see her, and he danced with no one else. He never took his eyes off her. But, before the dance was over, she slipped off, and home she went, and when the maids came back, once again, she pretended to be asleep with her cap o' rushes on.

The next day they said to her again, "Well, Cap o' Rushes, you should have been there to see the lady. There she was again, gay and grand, and the young master he never took his eyes off her."

"Well, there," said she, "I should have liked to have seen her."

"Well," said they, "there's a dance again this evening, and you must go with us, for she's sure to be there."

Come that evening, Cap o' Rushes said she was too tired to go, and do what they would she stayed at home. But when they were gone, she offed her cap o' rushes and cleaned herself, and away she went to the dance, like the night before.

The master's son was very glad indeed when he saw her. He danced with none but her and never took his eyes off her. When she wouldn't tell him her name, nor where she came from, he gave her a ring and told her if he didn't see her again he should probably die.

Well, before the dance was over, off she slipped, and home she went, and when the maids came home she was pretending to be asleep with her cap o' rushes on.

Well, next day they said to her, "There, Cap o' Rushes, you didn't come last night, and now you won't see the lady, for there's no more dances."

"Well, I should have really liked to have seen her," said she.

The master's son tried every way to find out where the lady had gone, but go where he might, and ask whom he might he never heard anything about her. Soon he got worse and worse for the love of her till he had to keep his bed.

"Make some gruel for the young master," they said to the cook. "He's dying for the love of the mysterious lady." The cook had just set about making it when Cap o' Rushes came in.

"What are you doing?" said she.

"I'm going to make some gruel for the young master," said the cook, "for he's dying for love of the mysterious lady."

"Let me make it," said Cap o' Rushes.

Well, the cook wouldn't let her at first, but at last she said yes, and Cap o' Rushes made the gruel. And when she had made it, she slipped the ring into it on the sly before the cook took it upstairs.

The young man drank it and then he saw the ring at the bottom.

"Send for the cook," he said immediately. So up she came.

"Who made this gruel here?" said he.

"I did," said the cook, for she was frightened. And he looked at her.

"No, you didn't," said he. "Say who did it, and you shan't be harmed."

"Well, then, 'twas Cap o' Rushes," said she.

"Send Cap o' Rushes here," said he.

So Cap o' Rushes came.

"Did you make my gruel?" said he.

"Yes, I did," said she.

"Where did you get this ring?" said he.

"From him that gave it to me," said she.

"Who are you, then?" said the young man.

"I'll show you," said she. And she took off her cap o' rushes, and there she was in her beautiful clothes.

Well, the master's son soon recovered, and they were to be married in a little time. It was to be a very grand wedding, and everyone was asked far and near. And Cap o' Rushes's father was asked. But she never told anybody who she was.

Before the wedding, she went down into the

kitchens and found the cook, and she said:

"This may seem an odd request. I want you to dress every dish without a grain of salt."

"That'll be nasty," said the cook.

"That doesn't matter," said she.

"Very well," said the cook.

Well, the wedding day came, and they were happily married. After the ceremony, all the company sat down to dinner. But when they began to eat the meat, it was so tasteless they couldn't eat it. Cap o' Rushes' father tried first one dish and then another, and then he burst out crying.

"What on earth is the matter?" said the master's son to him.

"Oh!" said he, "I had a daughter. And I asked her how much she loved me. And she said, 'As much as fresh meat loves salt.' And I turned her from my door, for I thought she didn't love me. And now I see she loved me best of all. And she may be dead for all I know."

"No, father, here she is!" said Cap o' Rushes. And she went up to him and put her arms round him. And so they lived happy ever after.

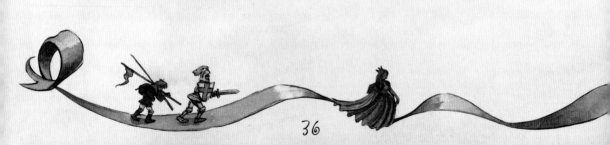

The Four Clever Brothers

By the Brothers Grimm

A poor man once said to his four sons, "Dear children, I have nothing to give you. You must go out into the wide world and try your luck. Begin by learning some craft or another, and see how you can get on."

So the four brothers took their walking sticks in their hands, and their little bundles on their shoulders, and after bidding their father goodbye, went out of the gate together. When they had gone some way they came to four crossways, each leading to a different country.

Then the eldest said, "Here we must part, but on this day in four years time we will come back to this spot, and in the meantime each must try to see what he can do for himself."

So each brother went his way, and as the eldest was hastening on he met a man, who asked him where he was going, and what he wanted.

"I am going to try my luck in the world, and should like to begin by learning some art or trade," answered he.

"Then," said the man, "Come with me, and I will teach you to become the most cunning thief that has ever been."

"No," said the other, "that is not an honest calling, and what can one look to earn but the gallows?"

"Oh!" said the man. "You need not fear the

gallows, for I will only teach you to steal what will be fair game. I meddle with nothing but what no one else can get or care anything about."

So the young man agreed to follow his trade, and he showed himself so clever, that nothing could escape him that he had once set his mind upon.

The second brother also met a man, who, when he found out what he was setting out upon, asked him what craft he meant to follow.

"I do not know," said he.

"Then come with me, and be a stargazer. It is a noble art, for nothing can be hidden when once you understand the stars." The plan pleased him much, and he soon became such a skilful stargazer, that when he had served out his time, and wanted to leave his master, he gave him a glass, and said, "With this you can see all that is passing in the sky and on earth, and nothing can be hidden from you."

The third brother met a huntsman, who took him with him, and taught him so well about hunting, that he became very clever in the craft of the woods.

When he left his master he gave him a bow, and said, "Whatever you shoot at with this bow you will be sure to hit."

The youngest brother likewise met a man who asked him what he wished to do. "Would not you like," said he, "to be a tailor?"

"Oh, no!" said the young man. "Not at all. Sitting cross-legged from morning to night, working backwards and forwards with a needle, that would never suit me."

"Oh!" answered the man. "That is not my sort of tailoring. Come with me, and you will learn quite another kind of craft from that."

Not knowing what better to do, he came into the plan, and began learning all about tailoring from the beginning.

When he left his master, he gave him a needle, and said, "You can sew anything with this, be it as soft as an egg or as hard as steel, and the joint will be so fine that no seam will be seen."

And after the space of four years, at the time agreed upon, the four brothers met at the four crossroads, and having welcomed each other, set off towards their father's home. When they saw him they each explained all that had happened to them, and how they had learned some new craft. Their father was amazed at what he heard and was eager to see their new skills in action.

So, one day, as they were sitting before the house under a very high tree, the father said, "I should like to test what each of you can do."

So he looked up above him, and said to the

second son, "At the top of this tree there is a chaffinch's nest, see if you can tell me just how many eggs there are in it."

The stargazer took his glass, looked up, and said quickly, "There are five eggs, Father."

"Now," said the father to the eldest son, "take away the eggs without letting the bird that is sitting upon them and hatching them know anything of what you are doing."

So the cunning thief nimbly climbed up the tree, and brought back to his father the five eggs from under the bird, and the chaffinch never saw or felt what he was doing, but kept sitting at its ease, unaware that it had lost its eggs.

Then the father took the eggs, and put one on each corner of the table, and the fifth in the middle, and he said to the huntsman, "Cut all the eggs in two pieces using only one shot."

The huntsman took up his bow, and with one shot struck all the five eggs, just as his father had wished him to do.

"Now comes your turn," said he to the young tailor, "sew the eggs and the young birds in them together again, so neatly that the shot shall have done them no harm."

Then the tailor took his needle, and sewed the eggs as he was told, and when he had done, the thief was sent to take them back to the chaffinch's nest. He swiftly put them under the bird without its knowing it.

Then the mother bird went on sitting, and hatched its eggs, and in a few days the chicks crawled out, and had only a little red streak across their necks, where the tailor had sewn them neatly back together.

"Well done, sons!" said the old man. "You have made good use of your time, and learnt something worth knowing, but I do not know which of you ought to have the prize. I wish that a time might come for you to turn your skill to some account!"

Not long after this there was a great bustle in the country, for the king's daughter had been carried off by a mighty dragon.

The king mourned over his loss day and night, and made it known that whoever brought his precious daughter back to him should have her for a wife. It was thought by everyone to be an impossible rescue mission.

But the four brothers said to each other, "Here is a chance for us, let us try what we can do."

And they agreed to see whether they could not set the princess free.

"I will soon find out where she is," said the stargazer, and he looked through his glass. He soon cried out, "I see her far off, sitting upon a rock in the sea, and I can spy the dragon, guarding her."

Then the stargazer went to the king, and asked for a ship for himself and his brothers, and they sailed together over the sea, till they came to the right place. There they found the princess sitting, as

the stargazer had said, on the rock, and the dragon
was lying asleep, with his head upon her lap.

"I dare not shoot at him," said the huntsman,
"for I should kill the princess also."

"Then I will try my skill," said the thief. They got
into a small boat and snuck up to the rock. The

thief quickly stole the princess away from under the dragon, who did not wake.

Then away they hastened with her, back towards the ship, but soon came the dragon roaring behind them through the air, for it awoke and missed the princess. When it got over the boat the huntsman shot it straight through the heart so that it fell down dead. They were still not safe, though, for it was such a great beast that in its fall it overset the boat, and they had to swim in the open sea upon a few planks. But the tailor stitched the pieces back together and they got back safely.

When they had brought the princess to her father there was great rejoicing, and he said to the brothers, "One of you shall marry her, but you must settle among yourselves which it is to be." There soon arose a quarrel, and the stargazer said, "If I had not found the princess out, all your skill would have been of no use, therefore she ought to be mine."

"Your seeing her would have been of no use," said

the thief, "if I had not taken her away from the dragon, therefore she ought to be mine."

"No, she is mine," said the huntsman, "for if I had not killed the dragon, it would, after all, have torn you and the princess into pieces."

"And if I had not sewn the boat together again," said the tailor, "you would all have been drowned."

The king said, "Each of you is right, and as all cannot have the young lady, the best way is for neither of you to have her. The truth is, there is somebody she likes a great deal better. To make up for your loss, I will give each of you half a kingdom."

The brothers agreed that this plan would be much better than quarrelling or marrying a lady who loved another. So they accepted, and lived happily for the rest of their days.

Tattercoats

By Flora Annie Steel

*I*n a magnificent palace by the sea there once dwelt a very rich old lord, who had neither wife nor children living and only one little granddaughter, whose face he had never seen in all her life. He hated her bitterly, because at her birth his favourite daughter died, and when the old nurse brought him the baby he swore that she might live or die as she liked, but he would never look on her face as long as she lived.

So he turned his back, and sat by his window

looking out over the sea, and weeping great tears for
his lost daughter, till his white hair and beard grew
down over his shoulders and twined round his chair
and crept into the chinks of the floor, and his tears,
dropping onto the window ledge, wore a channel
through the stone, and ran away in a little river to
the great sea. Meanwhile, his granddaughter grew
up with no one to care for her, or clothe her. Only
the old nurse, when no one was by, would
sometimes give her a dish of scraps from the
kitchen, or a torn petticoat from the rag-bag, while
the other servants of the palace would drive her
from the house with blows and mocking words,
calling her 'Tattercoats' and pointing to her bare feet
and shoulders, till she ran away, crying, to hide
among the bushes.

So she grew up, with little to eat or to wear,
spending her days out of doors, her only companion
a gooseherd, who fed his flock of geese on the
common. And this gooseherd was a merry little

chap, and when she was hungry, or cold, or tired, he would play to her so gaily on his little pipe, that she forgot all her troubles, and would fall to dancing with his flock of noisy geese for partners.

Now one day people told each other that the king was travelling through the land, and was to give a great ball to all the lords and ladies of the country in the town nearby, and that the prince, his only son, was to choose a wife from amongst the maidens in the company. In due time one of the royal invitations to the ball was brought to the palace by the sea, and the servants carried it up to the old lord, who still sat by his window, wrapped in his long white hair and weeping into the little river that was fed by his tears.

Royal invitation

Tattercoats

But when he heard the king's command, he dried his eyes and bade them bring shears to cut him loose, for his hair had bound him a prisoner, and he could not move. Then he sent for rich clothes and jewels, which he put on, and he ordered the servants to saddle the white horse with gold and silk, that he might ride to meet the king. He quite forgot he had a granddaughter to take to the ball.

Meanwhile Tattercoats sat by the kitchen door weeping, because she could not go to see the grand doings. And when the old nurse heard her crying she went to the lord of the palace, and begged him to take his granddaughter with him to the ball.

But he only frowned and told her to be silent, while the servants laughed and said, "Tattercoats is happy in her rags, playing with the gooseherd! Let her be – it is all she is fit for."

A second, and then a third time, the old nurse begged him to let the girl go with him, but she was answered only by black looks and fierce words, till she was driven from the room by the jeering servants, with blows and mocking words.

Weeping over her ill-success, the old nurse went to look for Tattercoats, but the girl had been turned from the door by the cook, and had run away to tell her friend the gooseherd how unhappy she was because she could not go to the king's ball.

Now when the gooseherd had listened to her story, he bade her cheer up, and proposed that they should go together into the town to see the king, and all the fine things, and when she looked sorrowfully down at her rags and bare feet he played a note or two upon his pipe, so gay and merry, that she forgot all about her tears and her troubles, and before she well knew, the gooseherd had taken her by the hand, and she and he, and the geese before them, were dancing down the road towards town.

Before they had gone very far a handsome young man, splendidly dressed, rode up and stopped to ask

the way to the castle where the king was staying, and when he found that they too were going, he got off his horse and walked beside them along the road.

"You seem merry folk," he said, "and will be good company."

"Good company, indeed," said the gooseherd, and played a new tune that was not a dance.

It was a curious tune, and it made the strange young man stare and stare and stare at Tattercoats till he couldn't see her rags – till he couldn't, to tell the truth, see anything but her beautiful face.

Then he said, "You are the most beautiful maiden in the world. Will you marry me?"

Then the gooseherd smiled to himself, and played sweeter than ever.

But Tattercoats laughed. "Not I," said she, "you would be finely put to shame, and so would I be, if you took a goose girl for your wife! Go and ask one of the great ladies you will see tonight at the king's ball, and do not flout poor Tattercoats."

But the more she refused him the sweeter the
pipe played, and the deeper the young man fell in
love, till at last he begged her to come that night at
twelve to the king's ball, just as she was, with the
gooseherd and his geese, in her torn petticoat and
bare feet, and see if he wouldn't dance with her
before the king and the lords and ladies, and present
her to them all, as his dear and honoured bride.

Now at first Tattercoats said she would not, but
the gooseherd said, "Take fortune when it comes,
little one."

So when night came, and the hall in the castle
was full of light and music, and the lords and ladies
were dancing before the king, just as the clock
struck twelve, Tattercoats and the gooseherd,
followed by his flock of noisy geese, hissing and
swaying their heads, entered at the great doors, and
walked straight up the ballroom, while on either
side the ladies whispered, the lords laughed, and the

king seated at the far end stared in amazement.

But as they came in front of the throne Tattercoats' lover rose from beside the king, and came to meet her. Taking her by the hand, he kissed her thrice before them all, and turned to the king.

"Father!" he said, for it was the prince himself, "I have made my choice, and here is my bride, the loveliest and sweetest girl in all the land!"

Before he had finished speaking, the gooseherd had put his pipe to his lips and played a few notes that sounded like a bird singing far off in the woods, and as he played, Tattercoats' rags were changed to shining robes sewn with glittering jewels, a golden crown lay upon her hair, and the flock of geese behind her became a crowd of dainty pages, bearing her long train. As the king rose to greet her as his daughter the trumpets sounded loudly in honour of the new princess, and the people outside in the street said to each other:

"Ah! Now the prince has chosen for his wife the

loveliest girl in all the land!"

But the gooseherd was never seen again, and no one knew what became of him, while the old lord went home once more to his palace by the sea, for he could not stay at court, when he had sworn never to look on his granddaughter's face.

So there he still sits by his window – if you could only see him – weeping more bitterly than ever. And his white hair has bound him to the stones, and the river of his tears runs away to the great sea.

The Clever Apprentice

By Walter Gregor

A shoemaker once engaged an apprentice. A short time after the apprenticeship began the shoemaker asked the boy what he would call him when addressing him.

"Oh, I would just call you master," answered the apprentice.

"No," said the master, "you must call me master above all masters."

Continued the shoemaker, "What would you call my trousers?"

Apprentice: "Oh, I would call them trousers."

Shoemaker: "No, you must call them struntifers. And what would you call my wife?"

Apprentice: "Oh, I would call her mistress."

Shoemaker: "No, you must call her the Fair Lady Permoumadam. And what would you call my son?"

Apprentice: "Oh, I would call him Johnny."

Shoemaker: "No, you must call him John the Great. And what would you call the cat?"

Apprentice: "Oh, I would call him pussy."

Shoemaker: "No, you must call him Great Carle Gropus. And what would you call the fire?"

Apprentice: "Oh, I would call it fire."

Shoemaker: "No, you must call it Fire Evangelist. And what would you call the peat stack?"

Apprentice: "Oh, I would just call it peat stack."

Shoemaker: "No, you must call it Mount Potago. And what would you call the well?"

Apprentice: "Oh, I would call it well."

Shoemaker: "No, you must call it the Fair Fountain. And, last of all, what would you call the house?"

Apprentice: "Oh, I would call it house."

Shoemaker: "No, you must call it the Castle of Mungo."

The shoemaker, after giving this lesson to his apprentice, told him that the first day he managed to use all these words at once, and was able to do so without making a mistake, the apprenticeship would be at an end.

The apprentice thought hard about the shoemaker's agreement, and was not long in making an occasion for using the words. One morning he got out of bed before his master and lit the fire. He then tied some bits of paper to the tail of the cat and threw the animal into the fire. The cat ran out with the papers all in a blaze, landed in the peat stack, which caught fire.

The Clever Apprentice

The apprentice hurried to his master and cried out, "Master above all masters, start up and jump into your struntifers, and call upon Sir John the Great and the Fair Lady Permoumadam, for Carle Gropus has caught hold of Fire Evangelist, and he is out to Mount Potago, and if you don't get help from the Fair Fountain, the whole of Castle Mungo will be burned to the ground!

The apprentice hurried to his master and cried out, "Master above all masters, start up and jump into your struntifers, and call upon Sir John the Great and the Fair Lady Permoumadam, for Carle Gropus has caught hold of Fire Evangelist, and he is out to Mount Potago, and if you don't get help from the Fair Fountain, the whole of Castle Mungo will be burned to the ground!"

Master above all masters, start up and jump into

The Wise Girl

By Katharine Pyle

There was once a girl who was wiser than the king and all his councillors. Her father was so proud of her that he boasted about her cleverness at home and abroad. He could not keep quiet about it. One day he was boasting to one of his neighbours, and he said, "The girl is so clever that not even the king could ask her a question she couldn't answer, or read her a riddle she couldn't unravel."

Now it so chanced the king was sitting at a window nearby, and he overheard what the girl's father was saying. The next day he sent for the man to come before him.

"I hear you have a daughter who is so clever that no one in the kingdom can equal her, and is that so?" asked the king.

Yes, the man said. Too much could not be said of her wit and cleverness.

That was well, and the king was glad to hear it. He had thirty eggs, they were fresh and good, but it would take a clever person to hatch chickens out of them. He then bade his chancellor get the eggs and give them to the man.

"Take these home to your daughter," said the king, "and bid her hatch them out for me. If she succeeds she shall have a bag of money, but if she fails you shall be beaten as a vain boaster."

The man was troubled when he heard this. Still his daughter was so clever he was almost sure she could hatch out the eggs. He carried them home to her and told her exactly what the king had said. It did not take the girl long to find out that the eggs had been boiled.

When she told her father, he made a great to-do. That was a pretty trick for the king to have played. Now he would have to take a beating and all the neighbours would hear about it. The girl, however, told him to be of good cheer. "Go to bed and sleep," said she. "I will think of some way out of the trouble. No harm shall come to you, even if I have to go to the palace myself and take the beating in your place."

The next day the girl gave her father a bag of boiled beans and told him to take them out to a certain place where the king rode by every day. "Wait until you see him coming," said she, "and then begin to sow the beans." At the same time he was to call out so loudly that the king could not help but hear him. The man took the bag of beans and went out to the field his daughter had spoken of. He waited until he saw the king coming, and then he began to sow the beans. At the same time he cried, "Come sun, come rain! Heaven grant that these boiled beans may yield a good crop."

The king was surprised that any one should be so stupid as to think boiled beans would grow and yield a crop. He did not recognize the man, and he stopped his horse to speak to him. "My poor man," said he, "how can you expect boiled beans to grow? Do you not know that is impossible?"

"Whatever the king commands should be possible," answered the man, "and if chickens can hatch from boiled eggs why should not boiled beans yield a crop?"

When the king heard this he looked at the man more closely, and then he recognized him as the father of the clever daughter.

"You have indeed a clever daughter," said he. "Take your beans home and bring me back the eggs I gave you."

The man was very glad when he heard that, and made haste to obey. He carried the beans home then took the eggs and brought them back to the king's palace.

After the king had received the eggs he gave the man a handful of flax. "Take this to your clever daughter," he said, "and bid her make for me within the week a full set of sails for a large ship. If she does this she shall receive half of my kingdom as a reward, but if she fails you shall have a beating that you will not soon forget."

The man returned home lamenting his hard lot.

"What is the matter?" asked his daughter. "Has the king set another task that I must do?"

Yes, that he had – her father showed her the flax the king had sent her and gave her the message.

"Do not be troubled," said the girl. "No harm shall come to you. Go to bed and sleep quietly, and tomorrow I will send the king an answer that will satisfy him."

The man believed what his daughter said. He went to bed and slept quietly.

The next day the girl gave her father a small piece of wood. "Carry this to the king," said she. "Tell him I am ready to make the sails, but first let him make me of this wood a large ship so that I may fit the sails to it."

The father did as the girl bade him, and the king was surprised at the cleverness of the girl in returning him such an answer.

"That is all very well," said he, "and I will excuse her from this task. But here! Here is a glass mug. Take it home to your clever daughter. Tell her it is my command that she dip out the waters from the ocean bed so that I can ride over the bottom dry shod. If she does this, I will take her for my wife, but if she fails you shall be beaten within an inch of your life."

The man took the mug and hastened home, weeping aloud and bemoaning his fate.

"Well, and what is it?" asked his daughter. "What does the king demand of me now?"

The man gave her the glass mug and told her what the king had said.

"Do not be troubled," said the girl. "Go to bed and sleep in peace. You shall not be beaten, and soon I shall be reigning as queen over all this land."

The man had trust in her. He went to bed and dreamed he saw her sitting by the king wearing a crown.

The Wise Girl

The next morning the girl gave her father a bunch of wool. "Take this to the king," she said. "Tell him that you have given me the mug, and I am willing to dip the sea dry, but first let him take this wool and stop up all the rivers that flow into the ocean."

The man did exactly as his daughter instructed him. He took the wool to the king and repeated what she had said word for word.

Then the king saw that the girl was indeed a clever one, and he sent for her to come before him.

She came just as she was, in her homespun dress and her rough shoes and with a cap on her head, but for all her mean clothing she was as pretty and fine as a flower, and the king was not slow to see it. Still he wanted to make sure for himself that she was as clever as her messages had been.

"Tell me," said he, "what sound can be heard the farthest throughout the world?"

"The thunder that echoes through heaven and

69

earth," answered the girl, "and your own royal commands that go from lip to lip."

This reply pleased the king greatly. "And now tell me," he said to the girl, "exactly what is my royal sceptre worth?"

"It is worth exactly as much as the power for which it stands," the girl replied.

The king was so well satisfied with the way the girl answered that he no longer hesitated, he was determined that she should be his queen, and that they should be married at once.

The girl had something to say to this, however. "I am but a poor girl," said she, "and my ways are not your ways. It may well be that you will tire of me, or that you may be angry with me sometime, and send me back to my father's house to live. Promise that if this should happen you will allow me to carry back with me from the castle the thing that has grown most precious to me."

The king was willing to agree to this, but the girl

was not satisfied until he had written down his promise and signed it with his own royal hand. Then she and the king were married with the greatest magnificence, and she came to live in the palace and reign over the land.

Now while the girl was still only a peasant she had been well content to dress in homespun and live as a peasant should, but after she became queen she would wear nothing but the most magnificent robes and jewels and ornaments, for that seemed to her only right and proper for a queen. But the king, who was of a very jealous nature, thought his wife did not care at all for him, but only for the fine things he could give her.

One day the king and queen were to ride abroad together, and the queen spent so much time in dressing herself that the king was kept waiting, and he became very angry. When she appeared before him, he would not even look at her. "You care nothing for me, but only for the jewels and fine clothes you wear!" he cried. "Take with you those that are the most precious to you, as I promised you, and return to your father's house. I will no longer have a wife who cares only for my possessions and not at all for me."

Very well, the girl was willing to go. "And I will be happier in my father's house than I was when I first met you," said she. Nevertheless she begged that she might spend one more night in the palace, and that she and the king might sup together once again before she returned home. To this the king agreed, for he still loved her, even though he was so angry with her.

So he and his wife supped together that evening, and just at the last the queen took a golden cup and filled it with wine. Then, when the king was not looking, she put a sleeping potion in the cup and gave it to him to drink. He took it and drank to the very last drop, suspecting nothing, but soon after he sank down among the cushions in a deep sleep.

Then the queen ordered him to be carried to her father's house and laid in the bed there.

When the king awoke the next morning he was very much surprised to find himself in the peasant's cottage. He raised himself upon his elbow to look about him, and at once the girl came to the bedside. He was surprised to see that she was again dressed in the coarse and common clothes she had worn before she was married.

"What means this?" said the king, "how did I come to be here?

"My dear husband," said the girl, "your promise was that if you ever sent me back to my father's house I might carry with me the thing that had become most precious to me in the castle. You are that most precious thing, and I care for nothing else unless it makes me pleasing in your sight."

Then the king could no longer feel jealous or angry. He clasped her in his arms, and they kissed each other tenderly.

The Wise Girl

That day they returned to the palace, and from then on the king and his peasant queen lived together in the greatest love and happiness.

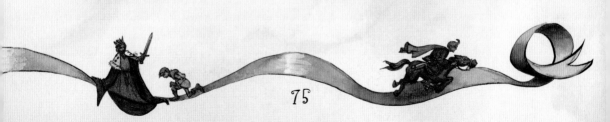

The Ogre's Bride

By Juliana Horatia Gatty Ewing

This story is set in a time when it was important for a girl to be a good housewife in order to find a husband. Girls were also expected to come with a dowry – a sum of money given to their new husband on the wedding day. Poor girls whose parents couldn't afford a dowry might have trouble finding a husband. But a cunning girl can usually find a way through such troubles – as Managing Molly did.

*I*n the days when ogres were still the terror of certain districts, there was one in particular who had long kept an entire neighbourhood in the grip of fear without anyone daring to challenge him.

The Ogre's Bride

By thefts and by heavy ransoms from merchants
too old and tough to be eaten, in one way and
another, the ogre had become very rich, and
although those who knew could tell of huge cellars
full of gold and jewels, and yards and barns
groaning with the weight of stolen goods, the richer
he grew the more anxious and greedy he became.
Day by day, he added to his stores, for though (like
most ogres) he was as stupid as he was strong, no
one had ever been found, by force or fraud, to get
the better of him.

What he took from the people was not their
heaviest grievance. Even to be killed and eaten by
him was not what they feared most. A man can die
but once, and if he is a sailor, a shark may eat him,
which is not so much better than being devoured by
an ogre. No, that was not the worst. The worst was
this – he would keep getting married. And as he
liked little wives, all the short women lived in fear
and dread. And as his wives always died very soon,

he was constantly courting fresh ones.

Some said he ate his wives, some said he tormented them, and others that he only worked them to death. Everybody knew it, and yet there was not a father who dared refuse his daughter if she were asked for. The ogre only cared for two things in a woman – he liked her to be little, and a good housewife.

Now, it was when the ogre had just lost his twenty-fourth wife (within the memory of man) that these two qualities were joined in the daughter of a certain poor farmer. He was so poor that he could not afford properly to give his daughter a dowry on her marriage, and so she had remained single. Everybody felt sure that Managing Molly must now be married to the ogre. The tall girls stretched themselves till they looked like maypoles, and said, "Poor thing!" The poor housekeepers gossiped from house to house, the heels of their shoes clacking as they went, and cried that this was what came of being too neat and careful.

And sure enough, the giant came to the farmer as he was in the field looking over his crops, and proposed to take Molly there and then. The farmer was so much put out that he did not know what he said in reply, either when he was saying it, or afterwards, when his friends asked about it. But he remembered that the ogre had invited himself to supper at the farm that day week.

Managing Molly did not distress herself at the news.

"Do what I bid you, and say as I say," said she to her father, "and if the ogre does not change his mind, you shall not come empty-handed out of the business."

By his daughter's desire the farmer now procured a large number of hares, and a barrel of white wine, which expenses completely emptied his slender moneybox, and on the day of the ogre's visit, she made a delicious and savoury stew with the hares in the biggest pickling tub, and the wine barrel was set on a bench near the table.

When the ogre came, Molly served up the stew, and the ogre sat down to sup, his head just touching the kitchen rafters. The stew was perfect, and there

was plenty of it to go around. For what Molly and her father ate was hardly to be counted in the tubful. The ogre was very pleased, and said politely:

"I'm afraid, my dear, that you have been put to great trouble and expense on my account, I have a large appetite, and like to sup well."

"Don't mention it, sir," said Molly. "The fewer rats there are, the more corn there is. How do you cook them?"

"Not one of all the extravagant women I have had as wives ever cooked them at all," said the ogre, and he thought to himself, 'Such a delicious stew out of rats! What frugality! What a housewife!'

When he broached the wine, he was no less pleased, for it was of the best.

"This must have cost you a great deal, neighbour," said he, drinking to the farmer as Molly left the room.

"I don't know that rotten apples could be better used," said the farmer, "but I leave all that to Molly.

Do you brew at home?"

"We give our rotten apples to the pigs," growled the ogre. "But things will be better organized when she is my wife."

The ogre was in great haste to arrange the match, and asked what dowry the farmer would give.

"I should never dream of giving a dowry with Molly," said the farmer, boldly. "Whoever gets her, gets dowry enough. On the contrary, I shall expect a good round sum from the man who deprives me of her. Our wealthiest farmer is just widowed, and therefore sure to be in a hurry for marriage. He would pay well for such a wife, I'll warrant."

"I'm no churl myself," said the ogre, who was anxious to secure his thrifty bride at any price, and he named a large sum of money, thinking, 'We shall live on rats henceforward, and the beef and mutton will soon cover the dowry.'

"Double that, and we'll see," said the farmer, stoutly. But the ogre became angry, and cried,

"What are you thinking of, man? Who is to stop me carrying your lass off, without 'with your leave' or 'by your leave,' dowry or none?"

"How little you know her!" said the farmer. "She is so firm that she would be cut to pieces sooner than give you any benefit of her thrift, unless you dealt fairly in the matter."

"Well," said the ogre, "let us meet each other." And he named a sum larger than he at first proposed, and less than the farmer had asked. The farmer agreed, as it was enough to make him prosperous for life.

"Bring it in a sack tomorrow morning," said he to the ogre, "and then you can speak to Molly, she's gone to bed now."

The next morning the ogre appeared, carrying the dowry in a sack, and Molly came to meet him.

"There are two things," said she, "I would ask of any husband of mine – a new farmhouse, built as I should direct, with a view to economy, and a feather bed of fresh goose feathers, filled when the old woman plucks her geese. If I don't sleep well, I cannot work well."

'That is better than asking for finery,' thought the ogre, 'and after all the house will be my own.'

To save the expense of labour, he built it himself, and worked hard, day after day, under Molly's orders, till winter came. Then it was finished.

"Now for the feather bed," said Molly. "I'll sew up the ticking, and when the old woman plucks her geese, I'll let you know."

When it snows, they say the old woman up in the sky is plucking her geese, and so at the first snow storm Molly sent for the ogre.

"You see the feathers falling," said she, "fill up the bed with them."

"How am I to catch them?" cried the ogre.

"Silly! Don't you see them lying there in a heap?" cried Molly, "get a shovel, and set to work."

The ogre carried in shovelfuls of snow to the bed, but as it melted as fast as he put it in, his labour never seemed done. Towards night the room got so cold that the snow would not melt, and the bed was soon filled. Molly hastily covered it with sheets and blankets, and said, "Pray rest here tonight, and tell me if the bed is not comfort itself. Tomorrow we will be married."

So the tired ogre lay down on the bed he had filled up, but, do what he would, he just could not get warm.

"The sheets must be damp," said he, and in the morning he woke with such horrible pains that he could hardly move, and half the bed had melted away. "It's no use," he groaned, "she's a managing woman, but to sleep on such a bed would be the death of me."

And the ogre went off home as quickly as he could, before Molly could call upon him to be married, for she was so managing that he was afraid of her already.

When Molly found that he had gone, she sent a messenger after him.

"What does he want?" cried the ogre.

"The bride is waiting for you," was the reply.

"Tell him I'm too ill to be married," said the ogre.

But the messenger soon returned.

"He says she wants to know what you will give her to make up for the disappointment."

"She's got the dowry, and the farm, and the feather-bed," groaned the ogre, "What more does she want?"

"She says you've pressed the feather bed flat, and she wants some more goose feathers."

"There are geese enough in the yard," yelled the

ogre, "Let the farmer drive them home."

The farmer, who overheard this order, lost no time in taking his leave, and as he passed through the yard he drove home the geese.

It is said that the ogre never recovered from his ordeal. As for Molly, being now well dowered, she had no lack of offers of marriage, and was soon wed to her content.

STRANGE AND MAGICAL TALES

The Broad Man, the Tall Man, and the Man with Eyes of Flame

By Alexander Chodsko

There was once a king of a certain country who had a daughter, who was not only exceedingly beautiful but also remarkably clever. Many kings and princes travelled from far distant

The Broad Man, the Tall Man, and the Man with Eyes of Flame

lands, each one with the hope of making her his wife. But she would have nothing to do with any one of them. Finally, it was proclaimed that she would marry the man who for three successive nights could keep such strict watch upon her that she could not escape unnoticed. Those who failed were to have their heads cut off.

The news of this offer spread to all parts of the world. A great many kings and princes hastened to make the trial, taking their turn and keeping watch. But each one lost his life in the attempt, for they could not prevent, indeed they were not even able to see, the princess take her flight.

Now it happened that Matthias, prince of a royal city, heard of what was going on and resolved to watch through the three nights. He was young, handsome as a deer and brave as a falcon. His father did all he could to turn him from his purpose – he used entreaties, prayers, threats, in fact he forbade him to go, but in vain, nothing could prevent him.

What could the poor father do? Worn out with contention, he was at last obliged to consent. Matthias filled his purse with gold, girded his best sword to his side, and quite alone started off to seek the fortune of the brave.

Walking along the next day, he met a man who seemed hardly able to drag one leg after the other.

"Where are you going?" asked Matthias.

"I am travelling all over the world in search of happiness."

"What is your profession?"

"I have no profession, but I can do what no one else can. I am called Broad, because I have the power of swelling myself to such a size that there is room for a whole regiment of soldiers inside me."

So saying he puffed himself out till he formed a barricade from one side of the road to the other.

"Bravo!" cried Matthias, delighted at this proof of his capacities. "By the way, would you mind coming with me? I, too, am travelling across the

The Broad Man, the Tall Man, and the Man with Eyes of Flame

world in search of happiness."

"If there is nothing bad in it I am quite willing," answered Broad. And they continued their journey together.

A little further on they met a very slender man, frightfully thin, and tall and straight as a column.

"Whither are you going, good man?" asked Matthias, filled with curiosity at his strange appearance.

"I am travelling about the world."

"To what profession do you belong?"

"To no profession, but I know something everyone else is ignorant of. I am called Tall, and with good reason. For without leaving the earth I can stretch out and reach up to the clouds. When I walk I clear a mile at each step."

Without more ado he lengthened himself out until his head was lost in the clouds, while he really cleared a mile with each step.

"I like that, my fine fellow," said Matthias.

"Come, would you not like to travel with us?"

"Why not?" replied he. "I'll come."

So they proceeded on their way together. While passing through a forest they saw a man placing tree trunks one upon another.

"What are you trying to do there?" asked Matthias, addressing him.

"I have Eyes of Flame," said he, "and I am building a pile here." So saying he fixed his flaming eyes upon the wood, and the whole was instantly set alight.

"You are a very clever and powerful man," said Matthias, "would you like to join our party?"

"Alright, I am willing."

The Broad Man, the Tall Man, and the Man with Eyes of Flame

So the four travelled along together. Matthias was overjoyed to have met with such gifted companions, and paid their expenses generously, without complaining of the enormous sum of money he had to spend on the amount of food Broad consumed.

After some days they reached the princess's palace. Matthias had told them the object of his journey, and had promised each a large reward if he was successful. They gave him their word to work with a will at the task that every one up till then had failed to accomplish. The prince bought them each a handsome suit of clothes, and when they were all presentable sent them to tell the king, the princess's father, that he had come with his attendants to watch the princess for three nights. But he took very good care not to say who he was, nor whence he had come.

The king received them kindly, and after hearing their request said: "Reflect well before engaging yourselves in this, for if the princess escapes you will have to die."

"We very much doubt her escaping from us," they replied, "but come what will, we intend to make the attempt and to begin at once."

"My duty was to warn you," replied the monarch, smiling, "but if you still persist in your resolution I myself will take you to the lady's apartments."

Matthias was dazzled at the loveliness of the royal maiden, while she, on her side, received the brilliant and handsome young man most graciously, not trying to hide how much she liked his good looks and gentle manner. Hardly had the king retired when Broad lay down across the threshold. Tall and the Man with Eyes of Flame placed themselves near the window, while Matthias talked with the princess, and watched her every movement attentively.

Suddenly she ceased to speak, then after a few moments said, "I feel as if a shower of poppies

The Broad Man, the Tall Man, and the Man with Eyes of Flame

were falling on my eyelids."

She lay down on the couch, pretending to sleep.

Matthias did not breathe a word. Seeing her asleep he sat down at a table near the sofa, leaned his elbows upon it, and rested his chin in the hollow of his hands. Gradually he felt drowsy and his eyes closed, as did those of his companions.

Now this was the moment the princess was waiting for. Quickly changing herself into a dove, she flew towards the window. If it had not happened that one of her wings touched Tall's hair he would not have awakened, and he would certainly never have succeeded in catching her if it had not been for the Man with Eyes of Flame, for as soon as he knew which direction she had taken, he sent such a glance after her, that is, a flame of fire, that in the twinkling of an eye her wings were burned, and having been thus stopped, she was obliged to perch on top of a tree. From there Tall reached her easily, and placed her in Matthias' hands, where she became a princess again. Matthias was just waking from his sleep.

Next morning and the morning after the king was greatly astonished to find his daughter sitting by the prince's side, but he was obliged to keep silent and accept facts as they were, at the same time entertaining his guests royally. At the approach of the third night he spoke with his daughter, and begged her to practise all the magic of which she was capable, and to act in such a way as to free him from the presence of intruders of whom he knew neither the rank nor the fortune.

As for Matthias, he used every means in his power to bring about a happy ending to such a hitherto successful undertaking. Before entering the princess's apartments he took his comrades aside and said, "There is but one more stroke of luck, and then we have succeeded. If we fail, do not forget that our four heads will roll on the scaffold."

"Come along," replied the three, "never fear, we

shall be able to keep good watch."

When they came into the princess's room they hastened to take up their positions, and Matthias sat down facing the lady. He would have much preferred to remain with her without being obliged to keep watch all the time for fear of losing her forever. Resolving not to sleep this time, he said to himself, "Now I will keep watch upon you, but when you are my wife I will rest."

At midnight, when sleep was beginning to overpower her watchers, the princess kept silent, and, stretching herself on the couch, shut her beautiful eyes as if she were really asleep.

Matthias, his elbows on the table, his chin in the palms of his hands, his eyes fixed upon her, admired her silently. But as sleep closes even the eyes of the eagle, so it shut those of the prince and his companions.

The princess, who all this time had been watching them narrowly and only waiting for this

99

moment, got up from her seat, and changing herself into a little fly, flew out of the window. Once free, she again changed herself into a fish, and falling into the palace well, plunged and hid herself in the depths of the water.

She would certainly have made her escape if, as a fly, she had not just touched the tip of the nose of the Man with Eyes of Flame. He sneezed, and opened his eyes in time to notice the direction in which she had disappeared. Without losing an instant he gave the alarm, and all four ran into the courtyard. The well was very deep, but that did not matter. Tall stretched himself to the depth, and searched in all the corners – but he was unable to find the little fish, and it seemed impossible that it could ever have been there.

The Broad Man, the Tall Man, and the Man with Eyes of Flame

"Now then, get out of that, I will take your place," said Broad.

And getting in at the top by the rim, he filled up all the inside of the well, stopping it so completely with his huge body that the water sprang out – but nothing was seen of the little fish.

"Now it is my turn," said the Man with Eyes of Flame. "I warrant I'll dislodge this clever magician."

When Broad had cleared the well of his enormous person the water returned to its place, but it soon began to boil from the heat of the eyes of flame. It boiled and boiled, till it boiled over the rim – then, as it went on boiling and rising ever higher and higher, a little fish was seen to throw itself out on the grass half cooked. As it touched the ground it again took the form of the princess.

Matthias went to her and kissed her tenderly.

"You have conquered, my master and husband," she said, "you have succeeded in preventing my escape. Henceforth I am yours, both by right of conquest and of my own free will."

The young man's courtesy, strength and gentleness, as well as his beauty, were very pleasing to the princess, but her father, the king, was not so ready to approve of her choice, and he resolved not to let her go with them.

But this did not trouble Matthias, who determined to carry her off, aided by his three comrades. They soon all left the palace.

The king was furious, and ordered his guards to follow them and bring them back under pain of death. Meanwhile Matthias, the princess and the three comrades had already travelled a distance of some miles. When she heard the steps of the pursuers she begged the Man with Eyes of Flame to see who they were. Having turned to look, he told her that a large army of men on horseback were advancing at a gallop.

"They are my father's guards," said she, "we shall have some difficulty in escaping them."

The Broad Man, the Tall Man, and the Man with Eyes of Flame

Seeing the horsemen draw nearer she took the veil from her face, and throwing it behind her in the direction of the wind, said, "I command as many trees to spring up as there are threads in this veil."

Instantly, in the twinkling of an eye, a high thick forest rose up between them. Before the soldiers had time to clear a pathway for themselves through this dense mass, Matthias and his companions had been able to get a great distance ahead. They even had time to take a little rest.

"Look," said the princess, "and see if they are still coming after us."

The Man with Eyes of Flame looked back, and replied that the king's guards were out of the forest and coming towards them with all speed.

"They will not be able to reach us," cried she. And she let fall a tear from her eyes, saying as she did so, "Tear, become a river."

At the same moment a wide river flowed between them and their pursuers, and before the latter had found means of crossing it, Matthias and his party were far on in front.

"Man with Eyes of Flame," said the princess, "look behind and tell me how closely we are followed."

"They are quite near to us again," he replied, "they are almost upon our heels."

"Darkness, cover them," said she.

At these words Tall drew himself up. He stretched and stretched and stretched until he reached the clouds, and there, with his hat he half covered the face of the sun. The side towards the soldiers was black as night, while Matthias and his party, lit up by the shining half, went a good way without hindrance.

When they had travelled some distance, Tall uncovered the sun, and soon joined his companions by taking a mile at each step. They were already in sight of Matthias' home, when they noticed that the royal guards were again following them closely.

"Now it is my turn," said Broad. "Go in safety, I will remain here. I shall be ready for them."

He quietly awaited their arrival, standing motionless, with his large mouth open from ear to ear. The royal army, who were determined not to turn back without having taken the princess, advanced towards the town at a gallop. They had decided among themselves that if it resisted they would lay siege to it.

Mistaking Broad's open mouth for one of the city gates, they all dashed through and disappeared.

Broad closed his mouth, and having swallowed

105

them, ran to rejoin his comrades in the palace of Matthias' father. He felt somewhat disturbed with a whole army inside him, and the earth groaned and trembled beneath him as he ran. He could hear the shouts of the people assembled round Matthias, as they rejoiced at his safe return.

"Ah, here you are at last, brother Broad," cried Matthias. "But what have you done with the army?"

"The army is here, quite safe," answered he, patting his enormous person. "I shall be very pleased to return them as they are, for the morsel is not very easy to digest."

"Let them out of their prison," said Matthias, enjoying the joke, and at the same time calling all the inhabitants to assist at the entertainment.

Broad, who looked upon it as a common occurrence, stood in the middle of the palace square, and putting his hands to his sides, began to cough. Then at each cough horsemen and horses fell out of his mouth, one over the other, plunging, hopping and jumping.

A few days later a splendid feast was given at the wedding of Prince Matthias and the princess. The king, her father, was also present. Tall had been sent to invite him. Owing to his knowledge of the road and the length of his limbs, he accomplished the journey so quickly that he was there before the royal horsemen had time to get back. It was well for them that it was so, for, had he not pleaded that their lives might be saved, their heads would certainly have been cut off for returning empty-handed.

Everything was now arranged to everybody's satisfaction. The princess's father was in the end delighted to know that his daughter was married to a gallant and noble prince, and Matthias generously rewarded his brave travelling companions, who remained with him to the end of their days.

107

Empty Bottles

By Howard Pyle

Nicholas Flamel was a real man who lived in the fifteenth century and had a reputation as a great alchemist. It was even said he had discovered the secrets of the Philosopher's Stone, which supposedly turns base metals into gold and grants eternal life. In Harry Potter and the Philosopher's Stone by J K Rowling, Nicholas Flamel is described as having worked with Professor Dumbledore.

*I*n the old, old days when men were wiser than they are in these times, there lived a great philosopher and magician, Nicholas Flamel. Not only did he know all the actual sciences, but the black arts as well, and magic, and what not. He conjured demons so that when someone passed a house on a moonlit night, they might see imps, great and small, little and big, sitting on the chimney stacks and the ridge-pole, clattering their heels on the tiles and chatting together.

He could change iron and lead into silver and gold, he discovered the elixir of life, and might have been living even to this day had he thought it worthwhile to do so.

There was a student at the university whose name was Gebhart, who was so well acquainted with algebra and geometry that he could tell at a single glance how many drops of water there were in a bottle of wine. As for Latin and Greek – he could patter them off like his A B Cs. Nevertheless, he was not satisfied with the things he knew, and wanted to learn the things that no schools could teach him. So one day he came knocking at Nicholas Flamel's door.

"Come in," said the wise man, and there Gebhart found him sitting in the midst of his books and bottles and diagrams and dust and chemicals and cobwebs, making strange figures upon the table with straws and a piece of chalk – for your true wise man can squeeze more learning out of straws and a piece of chalk than we common folk can get out of all the books in the world.

No one else was in the room but the wise man's servant, whose name was Babette.

"What is it you want?" said the wise man, looking at Gebhart over the rim of his spectacles.

"Master," said Gebhart, "I have studied day after day at the university, and from early in the morning until late at night, so that my head has hummed and my eyes were sore, yet I have not learned those things that I wish most of all to know – the arts that no one but you can teach. Will you take me as your pupil?"

The wise man shook his head.

"Many would like to be as wise as that," said he, "and few there be who can become so. Now tell me. Suppose all the riches of the world were offered to you, would you rather be wise?"

"Yes."

"Suppose you might have all the rank and power of a king or of an emperor, would you rather be wise?"

"Yes."

"Suppose I undertook to teach you, would you give up everything of joy and of pleasure to follow me?"

"Yes."

"Perhaps you are hungry," said the master.

"Yes," said the student, "I am."

"Then, Babette, bring some bread and cheese."

It seemed to Gebhart that he had learned all that Nicholas Flamel had to teach him.

It was the grey of dawn, and the master took the pupil by the hand and led him up the rickety stairs to the roof of the house, where nothing was to be seen but grey sky, high roofs and chimney stacks from which the smoke rose straight into the still air.

"Now," said the master, "I have taught you nearly all of the science that I know, and the time has come to show you the wonderful thing that has been waiting for us from the beginning when time was. You have given up wealth and the world and pleasure and joy and love for the sake of wisdom. Now, then, comes the last test – whether you can remain faithful to me to the end, if you fail in it, all is lost that you have gained."

After he said that, he stripped his cloak away

112

from his shoulders and laid bare the skin. Then he took a bottle of red liquor and began bathing his shoulder blades with it, and as Gebhart looked, he saw two little lumps bud out upon the smooth skin, and then grow and grow and grow until they became two great wings as white as snow.

"Now then," said the master, "take me by the belt and grip fast, for there is a long, long journey before us, and if you should lose your head and let go your hold you will fall and be dashed to pieces."

Then he spread the two great wings, and away he flew as fast as the wind, with Gebhart hanging to his belt.

Over hills, over dales, over mountains, over moors he flew, with the brown earth lying so far below that horses and cows looked like ants and men like fleas.

Then, by-and-by, it was over the ocean they were crossing, with the great ships that pitched and tossed below looking like wood chips in a puddle in rainy weather.

At last they came to a strange land, far, far away, and there the master landed upon a seashore where the sand was as white as silver. As soon as his feet touched the hard ground the great wings were gone like a puff of smoke, and the wise man walked like any other body.

At the edge of the sandy beach was a great, high, naked cliff, and the only way of reaching the top was by a flight of stone steps, as slippery as glass, cut in the solid rock.

The wise man led the way, and the student followed close at his heels, every now and then slipping and stumbling so that, had it not been for the help that the master gave him, he would have fallen more than once and have been dashed to pieces upon the rocks below.

At last they reached the top, and there found themselves in a desert, without a stick of wood or blade of grass, but only grey stones and skulls and

bones bleaching in the sun.

In the middle of the plain was a castle such as the eyes of man never saw before, for it was built all of crystal from roof to cellar. Around it was a high wall of steel, and in the wall were seven gates of polished brass.

The wise man led the way straight to the middle gate of the seven, where there hung a horn of pure silver, which he set to his lips. He blew a blast so loud and shrill that it made Gebhart's ears tingle. In an instant there sounded a great rumble and grumble like the noise of loud thunder, and the gates of brass swung slowly back.

But when Gebhart saw what he saw within the gates his heart crumbled away for fear, and his knees knocked together, for there, in the very middle of the way, stood a monstrous, hideous dragon, that blew out flames and clouds of smoke from its gaping mouth like a chimney on fire.

But the wise master was as cool as smooth water.

He thrust his hand into the bosom of his jacket and drew forth a little black box, which he flung straight into the fiery mouth.

Snap! The dragon swallowed the box.

The next moment it gave a great, loud, terrible cry, and, clapping and rattling its wings, leapt into the air and flew away, bellowing like a bull.

If Gebhart had been wonder-struck at seeing the outside of the castle, he was ten thousand times more amazed to see the inside thereof. For, as the master led the way and he followed, he passed through four-and-twenty rooms, each one more wonderful than the other. Everywhere was gold and silver and dazzling jewels that glistened so brightly that one had to shut one's eyes to their sparkle. Beside all this, there were silks and satins and velvets and laces and crystal and ebony and sandal-wood that smelled sweeter than musk and rose leaves. All the wealth of the world brought together into one place could not make such riches as Gebhart saw with his two eyes in these four-and-twenty rooms.

His heart beat fast within him.

At last they reached a little door of solid iron, beside which hung a sword with a blade that shone like lightning. The master took the sword in one hand and laid the other upon the latch of the door. Then he turned to Gebhart and spoke for the first time since they had started upon their long journey.

"In this room," said he, "you will see a strange thing happen, and in a little while I shall be as one dead. As soon as that comes to pass, go straight away through to the room beyond, where you will find upon a marble table a goblet of water and a silver dagger. Touch nothing else, and look at nothing else, for if you do all will be lost to both of us. Bring the water straight away, and sprinkle my face with it, and when that is done you and I will be the wisest and greatest men that ever lived, for I will make you equal to myself in all that I know. So now swear to do what I have just bid you, and not turn aside a hair's breadth in the going and the coming."

"I swear," said Gebhart, and crossed his heart.

Then the master opened the door and entered, with Gebhart close at his heels.

In the centre of the room was a great red cockerel, with eyes that shone like sparks of fire. As soon as it saw the master it flew at him, screaming fearfully, and spitting out darts of fire that blazed and sparkled like lightning.

It was a dreadful battle between the master and the cockerel. Up and down they fought, and here and there. Sometimes the student could see the wise man whirling and striking with his sword, and then again he would be hidden in a sheet of flame. But after a while he made a lucky stroke, and off flew the cockerel's head. Then, instead of a cockerel it was a great, hairy, black demon that lay dead on the floor.

But, though the master had conquered, he

looked like one sorely sick. He was just able to stagger to a couch that stood by the wall, and there he fell without breath or motion, like one dead, and as white as wax.

As soon as Gebhart had gathered his wits together he remembered what the master had said about the other room.

The door of it was also of iron. He opened it and passed within, and there saw two great tables or blocks of polished marble. Upon one was the dagger and a goblet of gold brimming with water. Upon the other lay the figure of a woman, and as Gebhart looked at her he thought her more beautiful than any thought or dream could picture. But her eyes were closed, and she lay like a lifeless figure of wax.

Empty Bottles

After Gebhart had gazed at her a long, long time, he took up the goblet and the dagger from the table and turned towards the door.

Then, before he left that place, he thought that he would have just one more look at the beautiful figure. So he did, and gazed and gazed until his heart melted away within him like a lump of butter, and, hardly knowing what he did, he stooped and kissed the lips.

Instantly he did so a great humming sound filled the whole castle, so sweet and musical that it made him tremble to listen. Then suddenly the figure opened its eyes and looked straight at him.

"At last!" she said. "Have you come at last?"

"Yes," said Gebhart, "I have come."

Then the beautiful woman arose and stepped down from the table to the floor, and if Gebhart thought her beautiful before, he thought her a thousand times more beautiful now.

"Listen," said she. "I have been asleep for

hundreds upon hundreds of years, for so it was fated to be until he should come who was to bring me back to life again. You are he, and now you shall live with me forever. In this castle is the wealth gathered by the king of the genii, and it is greater than all the riches of the world. It and the castle likewise shall be yours. I can transport everything to part of the world you choose, and can by my arts make you prince or king or emperor. Come."

"Stop," said Gebhart. "I must first do as my master bade me."

He led the way into the other room, the lady following him, and so they both stood together by the couch where the wise man lay. When the lady saw his face she cried out in a loud voice, "It is the great master! What are you going to do?"

"I am going to sprinkle his face with this water," said Gebhart.

"Stop!" said she. "Listen to what I have to say. In your hand you hold the water of life and the dagger of death. The master is not dead, but sleeping, if you sprinkle that water upon him he will awaken, young, handsome and more powerful than the greatest magician that ever lived. I myself, this castle, and everything that is in it will be his, and, instead of you becoming a prince or a king or an emperor, he will be so in your place. That, I say, will happen if he wakens. Now the dagger of death is the only thing in the world that has power to kill him. You have it in your hand. You have but to give him one stroke with it while he sleeps, and he will never waken again, and then all will be yours."

Gebhart neither spoke nor moved, but stood looking down upon his master. Then he set down the goblet very softly on the floor, and, shutting his eyes that he might not see the blow, raised the dagger to strike.

"That is all your promises amount to," said Nicholas Flamel the wise man. "After all, Babette, you need not bring the bread and cheese, for he

shall be no pupil of mine."

Then Gebhart opened his eyes.

There sat the wise man in the midst of his books and bottles and diagrams and dust and chemicals and cobwebs, making strange figures upon the table with straws and a piece of chalk.

And Babette, who had just opened the cupboard door for the loaf of bread and the cheese, shut it again with a bang, and went back to her spinning.

So Gebhart had to go back again to his Greek and Latin and algebra and geometry, for, after all, one cannot pour a gallon of beer into a quart pot, or the wisdom of a Nicholas Flamel into such a one as Gebhart.

As for the name of this story, why, if some promises are not bottles full of nothing but wind, there is little need to have a name for anything.

The Golden Snuff Box

By Flora Annie Steel

A snuff box was a little metal box, often beautifully decorated, used for carrying around snuff, which was powdered tobacco that some people used to sniff (or 'snuff') up their nose instead of smoking.

Once upon a time, and a very good time too, though it was not in my time, nor your time, nor for the matter of that in any one's time, there lived a man and a woman who had one son called Jack, and he was just terribly fond of reading books.

He read, and he read, and then, because his parents lived in a lonely house in a lonely forest and he never saw any other folk but his father and his mother, he became quite crazy to go out into the world and see charming princesses and the like.

So one day he told his mother he must be off, and she called him an air-brained addle-pate, but added that, as he was no use at home, he had better go seek his fortune.

Well, Jack hadn't gone far till he came to a field where his father was ploughing. Now although the man was dreadfully put out when he found his son was going away, he drew out of his pocket a little golden snuff box, and gave it to the lad, saying:

"If ever you are in danger of sudden death you may open the box, but not till then. It has been in our family for years and years, but, as we have lived, father and son, quietly in the forest, none of us have ever been in need of help – perhaps you may be."

So Jack pocketed the golden snuff box and went on his way. After a time, he grew very tired, and very hungry, and night closed in on him so that he could scarce see his way.

But at last he came to a large house and begged board and lodging at the back door. Now Jack was a good-looking young fellow, so the maid-servant at once called him in to the fireside and gave him plenty of good meat and bread and beer. And it so happened that while he was eating his supper the master's young daughter came into the kitchen and saw him. So she went to her father and said that there was the prettiest young fellow she had ever seen in the back kitchen, and that if her father loved her he would give the young man some employment. Now the gentleman of the house was exceedingly fond of his young daughter, and did not want to vex her, so he went into the back kitchen and questioned Jack as to what he could do.

"Anything," said Jack gaily, meaning, of course, that he could do any bit of work about the house.

But the gentleman saw a way of pleasing his young daughter and getting rid of the trouble of employing Jack, so he laughed and said, "If you can do anything, my good lad, you had better do this. By eight o'clock tomorrow morning you must have dug a lake four miles round in front of my mansion, and on it there must be floating a whole fleet of vessels. And they must range up in front of my mansion and fire a salute of guns. And the very last shot must break the leg of the four-post bed on which my daughter sleeps, for she is always late of a morning!"

Well! Jack was terribly flabbergasted, but he managed to say, "And if I don't do it?"

"Then," said the master of the house quite calmly, "you shall die."

So he bade the servants take Jack to a turret room and lock the door on him.

Well! Jack sat on the side of his bed and tried to think things out, but he found it so difficult. Soon he decided to think no more, and after saying his prayers he lay down and went to sleep. And he did sleep! When he woke it was close on eight o'clock, and he had only time to fly to the window and look out, when the great clock on the tower began to whirr before it struck the hour. And there was the lawn in front of the house all set with beds of roses and stocks and marigolds! Well! All of a sudden he remembered the little golden snuff box.

"I'm near enough to death," said he to himself, as he drew it out and opened it.

And no sooner had he opened it than out hopped three funny little red men in red nightcaps, rubbing their eyes and yawning, for they had been locked up in the box for years and years and years.

"What do you want, Master?" they said between their yawns. But Jack heard the clock whirring and knew that he hadn't a moment to lose, so he just gabbled off his orders. Then the clock began to strike, and the little men flew out of the window, and suddenly – Bang! Bang! Bang! Went the guns, and the last one must have broken the leg of the four-poster bed, for there at the window was the pretty young daughter in her nightcap, gazing with astonishment at the lake that was four miles round, with the fleet of vessels floating on it!

And so did Jack! He had never seen such a sight in his entire life, and he was quite sorry when the three little red men disturbed him by flying in at the window and scrambling into the golden snuff box.

"Give us a little more time when you want us next, Master," they said sulkily. Then they shut down the lid, and Jack could hear them yawning inside as they settled down to sleep.

The Golden Snuff Box

As you may imagine, the master of the house was astonished, while as for the young daughter, she declared at once that she would never marry anyone else but the young man who could do such wonderful things, the truth being that she and Jack had fallen in love with each other at first sight.

But her father was cautious. "It is true, my dear," said he, "that the young fellow seems a fine boy, but for all we know it may be chance, not skill, and he may have a broken feather in his wing. So we must try him again."

Then he said to Jack, "My daughter must have a fine house to live in. Therefore by tomorrow morning at eight o'clock there must be a magnificent castle standing on twelve golden pillars in the middle of the lake, and there must be a church beside it. And all things must be ready for the bride, and at eight o'clock precisely a peal of bells from the church must ring out for the wedding. If not, you will have to forfeit your life."

This time Jack intended to give the three little red men more time for their task, but what with having enjoyed himself so much all day, and having eaten so much good food, he overslept himself, so that the big clock on the tower was whirring before it struck eight when he woke, leapt out of bed and rushed to the golden snuff box.

But he had forgotten where he had put it, and so the clock had really begun to strike before he found it under his pillow, opened it, and gabbled out his orders. Then you never saw how the three little red men tumbled over each other and yawned and stretched and made haste all at one time, so

that Jack thought his life would surely be forfeit.
But just as the clock struck its last chime, out rang a
peal of bells, and there was the castle standing on
twelve golden pillars and a church beside it in the
middle of the lake. The castle was decorated for the
wedding, and there were crowds of servants and
retainers, all dressed in their Sunday best.

Never had Jack seen such a sight before, neither
had the gay young daughter who, of course, was
looking out of the next window in her nightcap.
And she looked so pretty and so gay that Jack felt
quite cross when he had to step back to let the three
little red men fly to their golden snuff box. But they
were far crosser than he was, and mumbled and
grumbled at the hustle, so that Jack was quite glad
when they shut the box down and began to snore.

Well, of course, Jack and the gay young daughter
were married, and were as happy as the day is long,
and Jack had fine clothes to wear, fine food to eat,
fine servants to wait on him, and as many fine

friends as he liked.

But it happened that one day when he was going hunting with all the ladies and gentlemen, Jack forgot to change the golden snuff box from his waistcoat pocket to that of his scarlet hunting coat, so he left it behind him. And what should happen but that the servant let it fall on the ground when he was folding up the clothes, and the snuff box flew open and out popped the three little red men yawning and stretching.

Well! When they found out that they hadn't really been summoned, and that there was no fear of death, they were in a towering temper and said they had a great mind to fly away with the castle, golden pillars and all.

On hearing this the servant pricked up his ears.

"Could you do that?" he asked.

"Could we?" they said, and they laughed loud. "Why, we can do anything."

Then the servant said ever so sharp, "Then move

this castle and all it contains right away over the sea where the master can't disturb us."

Now the little red men need not really have obeyed the order, but they were so cross with Jack that hardly had the servant said the words before the task was done, so when the hunting party came back, lo and behold! The castle, and the church, and the golden pillars had all disappeared!

At first all the rest set upon Jack for being a knave and a cheat, and, in particular, his wife's father threatened to kill for deceiving the merry young daughter, but at last he agreed to let Jack have twelve months and a day to find the castle and bring it back.

So off Jack started on a good horse with some money in his pocket. He travelled far and he travelled fast, and he travelled east and west, north and south, over hills and dales and valleys and mountains and woods, but never a sign of the missing castle did he see. Now at last he came to the palace of the king of all the mice in the wide world. And there was a little mousie in a fine shirt of mail armour and a steel cap doing sentry at the front gate, and he was not for letting Jack in until he had told his errand. And when Jack had told it, he passed him on to the next mouse sentry at the inner gate, so by degrees he reached the king's chamber, where he sat surrounded by mice courtiers.

Now the king of the mice received Jack very graciously, and said that he himself knew nothing of the missing castle, but, as he was king of all the mice in the whole world, it was possible that some of his subjects might know more than he. But the next morning, though there were brown mice, black mice, grey mice, white mice and piebald mice, from all parts of the world, they all answered with one breath, "If you please your majesty, we have not seen the missing castle."

Then the king said, "You must go and ask my elder brother the king of all the frogs. He may be able to tell you."

So Jack set off on the king's horse, and as he passed the outer gate he saw the little mouse sentry coming away, for its guard time was up. Now Jack was a kind-hearted lad, and he had saved some crumbs from his dinner in order to reward the little sentry for his kindness. So he put his hand in his pocket and pulled out the crumbs.

"Here you are, mousekin," he said. "That's for your trouble!"

Then the mouse thanked him kindly and asked if he would take him along to the king of the frogs.

"Not I," says Jack. "I should get into trouble with your king."

But the mousekin insisted. "I may be of some use to you," it said. So it ran up the horse's hind leg and up by its tail and hid in Jack's pocket. And the horse set off at a hard gallop, for it didn't like the mouse running over it.

So at last Jack came to the palace of the king of

all the frogs, and there at the front gate was a frog doing sentry in a fine coat of mail and a brass helmet. And the frog sentry was for not letting Jack in, but the mouse called out that they came from the king of all the mice and must be let in without delay. So they were taken to the king's chamber, where he sat surrounded by frog courtiers in fine clothes, but alas, he had heard nothing of the castle on golden pillars, and though he summoned all the frogs of all the world to a grand assembly next morning, they all answered his question with, "Kro kro, Kro kro," which means 'no' in frog language.

So the king said to Jack, "There remains but one thing. You must go and ask my eldest brother, the king of all the birds. His subjects are always on the wing, so perhaps they have seen something."

So Jack set off, and being a kind-hearted lad he gave the frog sentry, whom he met coming away from his guard, some crumbs leftover from dinner. The frog asked leave to go with him, and when Jack refused to take him he just gave one hop on to the stirrup, and a second hop on to the crupper, and the next hop he was in Jack's other pocket.

Then the horse galloped away like lightning, for it didn't like the slimy frog coming down 'plop' on its back.

Well, after a time, Jack came to the palace of the king of all the birds, and there at the front gate were a sparrow and a crow marching up and down with guns on their shoulders. Now at this Jack laughed fit to split, and the mouse and the frog from his pockets called out,

"We come from the king! Let us pass."

The sentries were amazed, and let them pass in without any delay.

When they came to the king's chamber, where he sat surrounded by all manner of birds, tomtits, wrens, cormorants, turtle-doves and the like, the king said he was sorry, but he had no news of the missing castle. And though he summoned all the birds of all the world to a grand assembly next morning, not one of them knew about it.

So Jack was quite disconsolate till the king said, "But where is the eagle? I don't see my eagle."

So two larks flew up into the sky till they couldn't be seen and sang ever so loud, till at last the eagle appeared.

Then the king said, "Have you seen a missing castle that stands upon twelve pillars of gold?"

And the eagle blinked its eyes and said, "Your majesty, that is where I've been."

Then everybody rejoiced, and when the eagle had eaten a whole calf so as to be strong enough for the journey, he spread his wide wings. Jack climbed on the eagle's back with the mouse in one pocket and the frog in the other, and they flew to the missing castle as quickly as possible.

And they flew over land and they flew over sea, until at last in the far distance they saw the castle standing on its twelve golden pillars. But all the

doors and windows were fast shut and barred, for, see you, the servant-master who had run away with it had gone out for the day hunting, and he always bolted doors and windows while he was absent lest someone else should run away with it.

Then Jack was puzzled to think how he should get hold of the golden snuff box, until the little mouse said:

"Let me fetch it. There is always a mouse-hole in every castle, so I am sure I shall be able to get in."

So it went off, and Jack waited on the eagle's wings till at last mousekin appeared.

"Have you got it?" shouted Jack, and the little mousie cried, "Yes!"

So every one rejoiced exceedingly, and they set off back to the palace of the king of all the birds, where Jack had left his horse, for now that he had the golden snuff box safe he knew he could get the castle back whenever he chose to send the three little red men to fetch it. But on the way over the sea, while Jack, who was dead tired with standing so long, lay down between the eagle's wings and fell asleep, the mouse and the eagle fell to quarrelling as to which of them had helped Jack the most, and they quarrelled so much that at last they laid the case before the frog. Then the frog, who made a very wise judge, said he must see the whole affair from the very beginning, so the mouse brought out the golden snuff box from Jack's pocket, and began to relate where it had been found and all about it. Now, at that very moment Jack awoke, kicked out his leg, and plump went the golden snuff box down to the very bottom of the sea!

"I thought my turn would come," said the frog, and went plump in after it.

Well, they waited, and waited, and waited for three whole days and three whole nights, but froggie never came up again, and they had just given him up in despair when his nose showed above the water.

"Have you got it?" they shouted.

"No!" says he, with a great gasp.

"Then what do you want?" they cried in a rage.

"My breath," says froggie, and with that he sinks down again.

Well, they waited two days and two nights more, and at last up comes the little frog with the golden snuff box in its mouth.

Then they all rejoiced exceedingly, and the eagle flew ever so fast to the palace of the king of the birds, and Jack was allowed to ride home.

But the year and a day that he had been allowed was almost gone, and even his gay young wife, after almost weeping her eyes out after her handsome young husband, had given up Jack for lost, so everyone was astounded to see him, and not over-pleased either to see him come without his castle. Indeed his father-in-law swore with many oaths that if it were not in its proper place by eight o'clock next morning Jack's life should be forfeit.

The Golden Snuff Box

Now this, of course, was exactly what Jack had wanted and intended from the beginning, because when death was nigh he could open the golden snuff box and order about the little red men. But he had opened it so often of late and they had become so cross that he was in a stew what to do, whether to give them time to show their temper, or to hustle them out of it. At last he decided to do half and half. So just as the hands of the clock were at five minutes to eight he opened the box, and stopped his ears!

Well! You never heard such a yawning, and scolding, and threatening, and blustering. What did he mean by it? Why should he take four bites at one cherry? If he was always in fear of death why didn't he die and have done with it?

In the midst of all this the tower clock began to whirr.

"Gentlemen!" said Jack – he was really quaking with fear, "Do as you are told."

145

"For the last time," they shrieked. "We won't stay and serve a master who thinks he is going to die every day."

And with that they flew out of the window – and they never came back.

The golden snuff box remained empty for evermore.

But when Jack looked out of window there was the castle in the middle of the lake on its twelve golden pillars, and there was his young wife ever so pretty and gay in her nightcap looking out of the window too.

So they lived happily ever after.

The Three Aunts

By George Webbe Dasent

*O*nce upon a time there was a poor man who lived in a hut far away in the wood. He made his living by shooting. He had an only daughter, who was very pretty, and as she had lost her mother when she was a child, and was now half grown up, she said she would go out into the world and earn her bread.

"Well, lassie!" said the father to his daughter. "True enough you have learned nothing here apart from how to pluck birds and roast them, but still you may as well try to earn your bread."

So the girl went off to seek a place, and when she had gone a little while, she came to a palace. There she stayed and got a place, and the queen liked her so well that all the other maids grew envious of her. So they made up their minds to tell the queen how the lassie said she could spin a pound of flax in four-and-twenty hours, for you must know the queen was a great housewife, and thought much of good work.

"Have you said this? Then you shall do it," said the queen, "but you may have a little longer."

Now, the poor lassie dared not say she had never spun in all her life, but she only begged for a room to herself. That she got, and the wheel and the flax were brought up to her. There she sat sad and weeping, and knew not how to help herself. She pulled the wheel this way and that, and twisted and turned it about, but she made a poor hand of it, for she had never even seen a spinning wheel in her life.

But all at once, as she sat there, in came an old woman to her.

"What ails you, child?" she said.

"Ah!" said the lassie, with a deep sigh. "It's no good to tell you, for you'll never be able to help me."

"Who knows?" said the old wife. "Maybe I know how to help you after all."

'Well', thought the lassie to herself, 'I may as well tell her', and so she explained how fellow-servants had said she could spin a pound of flax in four-and-twenty hours.

"And here am I, wretch that I am, shut up to spin all that heap in a day and a night, when I have never ever seen a spinning wheel in all my days."

"Well never mind, child," said the old woman. "If you'll call me aunt on the happiest day of your life, I'll spin this flax for you, and so you may just go away and lie down to sleep."

Yes, the lassie was willing enough, and off she went and lay down to sleep.

149

Next morning when she awoke, there lay all the flax spun on the table, and that so clean and fine, no one had ever seen such even and pretty yarn.

The queen was very glad to get such nice yarn, and she set greater store by the lassie than ever. But the rest were still more envious, and agreed to tell the queen how the lassie had said she could weave the yarn she had spun in four-and-twenty hours. So the queen said again, as she had said it she must do it – but if she couldn't quite finish it in four-and-twenty hours, she wouldn't be too hard upon her, she might have a little more time. This time, too, the lassie dared not say no, but begged for a room to herself, and then she would try. There she sat again, sobbing, and not knowing which way to turn, when another old woman came in and asked:

"What ails you, child?"

At first the lassie wouldn't say, but at last she told her the whole story of her grief.

"Well, well!" said the old wife. "Never mind. If you'll call me aunt on the happiest day of your life, I'll weave this yarn for you, and so you may just be off, and lie down to sleep." Yes, the lassie was willing enough, so she went away and lay down to sleep. When she awoke, there lay the piece of linen on the table, woven so neat and close, no weave could be better. So the lassie took the piece and ran down to the queen, who was very glad to get such beautiful linen, and set greater store than ever by the lassie. But as for the others, they grew still more bitter against her, and thought of nothing but how to find out something to tell about her.

At last they told the queen the lassie had said she could make up the piece of linen into shirts in four-and-twenty hours. Well, all happened as before, the lassie dared not say she couldn't sew, so she was shut up again in a room by herself, and there she sat in tears and grief. But then another old wife came, who said she would sew the shirts for her if she would call her aunt on the happiest day of her life. The lassie was glad to do this. She did as the old wife told her, and went and lay down to sleep.

Next morning when she woke she found the piece of linen made up into shirts. Such beautiful work no one had ever set eyes on, and more than that, the shirts were all marked and ready for wear. When the queen saw the work, she was so glad that she clapped her hands, and said:

"Such sewing I never had, nor even saw, in all my born days," and after that she was as fond of the lassie as of her own children, and she said to her:

"Now, if you would like to have the prince for

your husband, you shall have him, for you will never need to hire work-women. You can sew, and spin, and weave all yourself."

So as the lassie was pretty, and the prince was glad to have her, the wedding soon came on. But just as the prince was going to sit down with the bride to the bridal feast, in came an ugly old hag with a long nose. So up got the bride and made a curtsey, and said, "Good day, Auntie."

"That is an auntie to my bride?" said the prince.

"Yes, she is!"

"Well, then, she'd better sit down with us to the feast," said the prince, but to tell you the truth, he thought she was a loathsome woman.

But just then in came another ugly old hag. She had a back so humped and broad, she had hard work to get through the door. Up jumped the bride, and she greeted her with, "Good day, Auntie!"

And the prince asked again if that were his bride's aunt. They both said yes, so the prince said that she too had better sit down with them.

Then another ugly old hag came in, with eyes as large as saucers, and so red and bleary, it was gruesome to look at her. But up jumped the bride again, and said, "Good day, Auntie."

The prince asked her to sit down, then asked, "How can my bride have such misshapen aunties?"

The Three Aunts

"I'll tell you why," said the first. "I was just as good-looking when I was her age, but I was always kept sitting, and poking, and nodding over my spinning, and so my nose got stretched and stretched, until it got as long as you now see it."

"And I," said the second, "ever since I was young, I have sat and scuttled backwards and forwards over my loom, and that's how my back has got so broad and humped as you now see it."

"And I," said the third, "ever since I was little, I have sat and stared and sewn, and sewn and stared, night and day, and that's why my eyes have got so ugly and red, and now there's no help for them."

"So!" said the prince, "'twas lucky I came to know this, for if folk can get so misshapen by all this, then my bride shall neither spin, nor weave, nor sew all her life long."

The Husband of the Rat's Daughter

By Andrew Lang

*O*nce upon a time there lived in Japan a rat and his wife who came from an old and noble race. They had one daughter, the loveliest girl in all the rat world. Her parents were very proud of her, and spared no pains to teach her all she ought to know. There was not another young lady in the whole town who was as clever as she was in gnawing through the hardest wood, or who could drop from such a height onto a bed, or run away so fast if anyone was heard coming. Great attention, too, was paid to her personal appearance, and her skin shone like satin, while her teeth were as white as pearls, and beautifully pointed.

Of course, with all these precious advantages, her parents expected her to make a brilliant marriage, and, as she grew up, they began to look round for a suitable husband.

But here a difficulty arose – the mother and father rat had very different ideas on who their daughter should marry.

The father was a rat from the tip of his nose to the end of his tail, outside as well as in, and he desired that his daughter should wed among her own people. She had no lack of suitors, but her father's secret hopes rested on a fine young rat, who had a moustache that almost swept the ground, and whose family was still nobler and more ancient than his own.

The mother had other views for her precious child. She was one of those people who always despised their own family and surroundings, and take pleasure in thinking that they themselves are made of finer material than the rest of the world. She thought highly of herself, and her daughter.

"*My* daughter should never marry a mere rat," she declared, holding her head high. "With her beauty and talents she had a right to look for someone a little better than *that*."

So she talked to anyone that would listen to her. What the girl herself thought about the matter nobody knew or cared – it was not the fashion in the rat world.

Many were the quarrels that the old rat and his wife had upon the subject, and sometimes they bore on their faces certain marks that looked as if they had not kept to words only.

"Reach up to the stars is *my* motto," cried the mother rat one day, when she was in a greater passion than usual. "My daughter's beauty places her higher than anything upon earth," she cried, "and I am certainly not going to accept a son-in-law who is beneath her."

"Better offer her in marriage to the sun," answered her husband impatiently. "As far as I know there is nothing greater than he."

"Well, I *was* thinking of it," replied the wife, "and as you are of the same mind, we will pay him a visit tomorrow."

So the next morning, the two rats, having spent hours in making themselves smart, set out to see the sun, leading their daughter between them. She had no say in the matter.

The journey took some time, but at length they came to the golden palace where the sun lived.

"Noble king," began the mother rat, "behold our daughter! She is so beautiful that she is above everything in the whole world. Naturally, we wish for a son-in-law who, on his side, is greater than all.

Therefore we have come to you."

"I feel very much flattered," replied the sun, who was so busy that he had not the least wish to marry anybody. "You do me great honour by your proposal. Only, in one point you are mistaken, and it would be wrong of me to take advantage of your ignorance. There is something greater than I am, and that is the cloud. Look!" And as he spoke a cloud spread itself over the sun's face, blotting out his rays.

"Oh, well, we will speak to the cloud," said the mother. And turning to the cloud she repeated her marriage proposal.

"Indeed I am unworthy of anything so charming," answered the cloud, "but you make a mistake again in what you say. There is one thing that is even more powerful than I, and that is the wind. Ah, here he comes, you can see for yourself."

And she *did* see, for catching up the cloud as he passed, he threw it on the other side of the sky.

Then, tumbling father, mother and daughter down to the earth again, he paused for a moment beside them, his foot on an old wall.

When she had recovered her breath, the mother began her little speech once more.

"The wall is the proper husband for your daughter," answered the wind, whose home consisted of a cave, which he only visited when he was not rushing about elsewhere. "You can see for yourself that he is greater than I, for he has power to stop me in my flight." And so the mother turned at once to the wall.

Then something happened that was quite unexpected by everyone.

"I won't marry that ugly old wall, which is as old as my grandfather," sobbed the girl, who had not uttered one word all this time. "I would have married the sun, or the cloud, or the wind, because it was my duty, although I love the handsome young rat, and him only. But that horrid old wall? No!"

And the wall, rather hurt, declared that he had no claim to be the husband of so beautiful a girl.

"It is quite true," he said, "that I can stop the wind who can part the clouds who can cover the sun, but there is someone who can do more than all these, and that is the rat. It is the rat who passes through me, and can reduce me to powder, simply with his teeth. If, therefore, you want a son-in-law who is greater than the whole world, seek him among the rats."

"Ah, what did I tell you?" cried the father. And his wife, though for the moment angry at being beaten, soon thought that a rat son-in-law was what she had always desired.

So all three returned happily home, and the wedding was celebrated three days after.

163

The Swineherd

By Hans Christian Andersen

*T*here was once a poor prince who possessed a kingdom which, though small, was yet large enough for him to marry on, and married he wished to be.

Now it was certainly a little audacious of him to venture to say to the emperor's daughter, "Will you marry me?" But he did venture to say so, for his name was known far and wide. There were hundreds of princesses who would gladly have said yes, but would she say the same?

The Swineherd

Well, we shall see. On the grave of the prince's father grew a rose tree, a very beautiful rose tree. It only bloomed every five years, and then bore but a single rose, but oh, such a rose! Its scent was so sweet that when you smelt it you forgot all your cares and troubles. And he had also a nightingale that could sing as if all the beautiful melodies in the world were shut up in its little throat. This rose and this nightingale the princess was to have, and so they were both put into silver caskets and sent to her.

The emperor had them brought to him in the great hall, where the princess was playing 'Here comes a duke a-riding' with her ladies-in-waiting. And when she caught sight of the big caskets that contained the presents, she clapped her hands.

"If only it were a little pussycat!" she said. But the rose tree with the beautiful rose came out.

"But how prettily it is made!" said all the ladies-in-waiting.

"It is more than pretty," said the emperor.

But the princess felt it, and then she almost began to cry.

"Ugh! Papa," the princess said, "it is not artificial, it is *real*!"

"Ugh!" said all the ladies-in-waiting, "it is real!"

"Let us see first what is in the other casket before we begin to be angry," said the emperor, and there came out the nightingale. It sang so beautifully that one could scarcely utter a cross word against it.

"*Superbe*! *Charmant*!" said the ladies-in-waiting, for they all chattered French, each one worse than the other.

"How much the bird reminds me of the musical snuff box of the late empress!" said an old courtier. "Ah, yes, it is exactly the same tone, precisely the same execution!"

"Yes," said the emperor, and then he wept.

The Swineherd

"I hope that this, at least, is not real?" asked the princess.

"Yes, it is," said those who had brought it.

"Then let the real bird fly away," said the princess, and she would not on any account allow the prince to come.

But he was not daunted. He dirtied his face with mud, drew his cap well over his face, and knocked at the door. "Good day, emperor," he said. "Can I get a place here as servant in the castle?"

"Yes," said the emperor, "but there are so many who ask for a place that I don't know whether there will be one for you, but, still, I will think of you. Stay, it has just occurred to me that I want someone to look after the swine, for I have many of them."

And the prince got the job of imperial swineherd. He had a wretched little room close to the pigsties. Here he had to stay, but the whole day he sat working, and when evening came he had made a pretty little pot. All round it were little bells, and when the pot boiled they jingled most beautifully and played the tune:

> *"Where is Augustus dear?*
> *Alas! He's not here, here, here!"*

But the most wonderful and intriguing thing was, that when one held one's finger in the steam of the pot, then at once one could smell what dinner was ready in any fireplace in the town. How about that! That was indeed something quite different from the rose.

Now the princess came walking past with all her ladies-in-waiting, and when she heard the tune she stood still and her face beamed with joy, for she also could play 'Where is Augustus dear?'

It was the only tune she knew, but that she could play with one finger.

"Why, that is what I play!" she said. "He must be a most accomplished swineherd! Listen! Go down and ask him what the instrument costs."

And one of the ladies-in-waiting went down, but she put on wooden clogs because of the mud. "What will you take for the pot?" she asked.

"I will have ten kisses from the princess," said the swineherd.

"Oh my, heaven forbid!" said the lady-in-waiting.

"Yes, I will sell it for nothing less," replied the swineherd.

"What did he say?" asked the princess urgently, when the lady-in-waiting returned.

"I should hardly like to tell you," answered the lady-in-waiting. The princess insisted, however, and her lady told her of the swineherd's request.

"He is disobliging!" said the princess. But she had only gone a few steps when the bells rang out so prettily:

"Where is Augustus dear?
Alas! He's not here, here, here."

169

"Listen!" said the princess. "'Ask him whether he will take ten kisses from my ladies-in-waiting."

"No, thank you," said the swineherd. "Ten kisses from the princess, or else I keep my pot."

"That is very tiresome!" said the princess, but she said to the ladies-in-waiting, "You must put yourselves in front of me, so no one can see."

And so the ladies-in-waiting placed themselves in front and then spread out their dresses, so the swineherd got his ten kisses from the princess, and she got the pot.

What happiness that was! The whole night and the whole day the pot was made to boil. There was not a fireplace in the whole town where they did not know what was being cooked, whether it was at the chancellor's or at the shoemaker's.

The ladies-in-waiting danced together and clapped their hands.

"We know who is going to have soup and pancakes, we know who is going to have porridge and sausages – isn't it interesting?'

"Yes, very interesting!" said the first lady-in-waiting.

"But don't say anything about it, for I am the emperor's daughter."

"Oh, no, of course we won't!" said everyone.

The swineherd – that is to say, the prince (though they did not know he was anything but a true swineherd) – let no day pass without making something, and one day he made a rattle which, when it was turned round, played all the waltzes and polkas that had ever been known.

"But that is *superbe*!" said the princess as she

passed by. "I have never heard a more beautiful composition. Listen! Go down and ask him what this instrument costs, but I won't kiss him again."

"He wants a hundred kisses from the princess," said the lady-in-waiting who had gone down to ask the swineherd.

"He is mad!" said the princess, and then she went on, but she had only gone a few steps when she stopped, and turned.

"One ought to encourage art," she said. "I am the emperor's daughter! Tell him he shall have, as before, ten kisses, the rest he can take from my ladies-in-waiting."

"But we don't at all like being kissed by him," said the ladies-in-waiting.

"That's nonsense," said the princess, "and if I can kiss him, you can too. Besides, remember that I give you board and lodging."

So the ladies-in-waiting had to go down to speak to the swineherd again.

The Swineherd

"A hundred kisses from the princess," said he, "or each keeps his own."

"Put yourselves in front of us," she said then, and so all the ladies-in-waiting put themselves in front, and he began to kiss the princess.

"What can that commotion be by the pigsties?" asked the emperor, who was standing on the balcony. He put on his spectacles to see clearer.

"Why those are the ladies-in-waiting playing their silly games. I must go down to them and stop such nonsense."

So he took off his shoes, which were shoes though he had trodden them down into slippers. What a hurry he was in, to be sure!

As soon as he came into the yard he walked very softly, and the ladies-in-waiting were so busy counting the kisses and seeing fair play that they never noticed the emperor.

"What is going on?" he said. He threw one of his slippers at their heads just as the swineherd was taking his eighty-sixth kiss.

"Be off with you!" said the emperor, for he was very angry. And so the princess and the swineherd were driven out of the empire.

Soon after, the princess wept, the swineherd was scolding, and the rain was streaming down. "Alas, what an unhappy creature I am!" sobbed the princess. "If only I had taken the beautiful prince! Alas, how unfortunate I am!"

And the swineherd went behind a tree, washed his muddy face, threw away his old clothes, and then stepped forwards in his splendid dress, looking so beautiful that the princess was obliged to curtsey. "I now come to this. I despise you!" he said. "You would have nothing to do with a noble prince, you did not understand the rose or the nightingale, but you would kiss the swineherd for a toy. This is what you get for it!" And he went into his kingdom and shut the door in her face, and she had to stay outside singing:

"Where's my Augustus dear?
Alas! He's not here, here, here!"

175

ALONG THE ROAD

Hans in Luck

By Joseph Jacobs

Some men are born to good luck – all they do or try to do comes right and all that falls to them is gain, all their geese are swans and all their cards are trumps. Toss them which way you will, they will always, like poor puss, alight upon their legs, and only move on so much the faster. The world may very likely not always think of them as they think of themselves, but what care they for the world? What can it know about the matter?

One of these lucky beings was neighbour Hans.

Hans in Luck

Seven years he had worked hard for his master. At last he said, "Master, my time is up, I must go home and see my poor mother once more – so pray pay me my wages and let me go." And the master said, "You have been a faithful servant, Hans, so your pay shall be handsome." He gave him a lump of silver as big as his head.

Hans took out his handkerchief, put the piece of silver into it, threw it over his shoulder, and jogged off on his road homewards. As he went lazily on, dragging one foot after another, a man came in sight, trotting gaily along on a capital horse. "Ah!" said Hans aloud. "What a fine thing it is to ride on horseback! There he sits as easy and happy as if he was at home, in the chair by his fireside. He trips against no stones, saves shoe leather, and gets on he hardly knows how."

Hans did not speak quietly, so the horseman heard it all, and said, "Well, friend, why do you go on foot then?"

"Ah!" said he, "I have this load to carry. To be sure it is silver, but it is so heavy that I can't hold up my head, and you must know it hurts my shoulder."

"What do you say of making an exchange?" said the horseman. "I will give you my horse, and you shall give me the silver, which will save you a great deal of trouble in carrying such a heavy load about with you."

"With all my heart," said Hans, "but as you are so kind to me, I must tell you one thing – you will have a weary task to draw that silver about with you."

However, the horseman got off, took the silver, helped Hans up, gave him the bridle into one hand and the whip into the other, and said, "When you want to go very fast, smack your lips loudly together, and cry 'Jip!'"

Hans was delighted as he sat on the horse, drew himself up, squared his elbows, turned out his toes, cracked his whip and rode merrily off, one minute whistling a merry tune, and another singing.

After a time he thought he should like to go a little faster, so he smacked his lips and cried, "Jip!" Away went the horse full gallop, and before Hans knew what he was about, he was thrown off, and lay on his back by the roadside. His horse would have run off, if a shepherd who was coming by, driving a cow, had not stopped it.

Hans soon came to himself, and got upon his legs again, sadly vexed, and said to the shepherd, "This riding is no joke, when a man has the luck to get upon a beast like this that stumbles and flings him off as if it would break his neck. However, I'm off now once and for all. I like your cow now a great deal better than this smart beast that played me this trick, and has spoiled my best coat, you see, in this puddle, which, by the by, smells not very like a nosegay. One can walk along at one's leisure behind that cow – keep good company, and have milk, butter, and cheese, every day, into the bargain. What would I give to have such a prize!"

"Well," said the shepherd, "if you are so fond of her, I will change my cow for your horse. I like to do good to my neighbours."

"Done!" said Hans, merrily. 'What a noble heart that good man has!' thought he. Then the shepherd jumped upon the horse, wished Hans and the cow good morning, and away he rode.

Hans brushed his coat, wiped his face and hands, rested a while, and then drove off his cow quietly, and thought his bargain a very lucky one. "If I have only a piece of bread (and I shall always be able to get that) I can eat my butter and cheese with it, and when I am thirsty I can milk my cow and drink the milk. What more can I wish for?"

When he came to an inn, he halted, ate up all his bread, and gave away his last penny for a glass of beer. When he had rested himself he set off again, driving his cow towards his mother's village. But the heat grew greater as soon as noon came on, till at last, as he found himself on a wide heath that would take him more than an hour to cross, he began to feel so hot and parched that his tongue stuck to the roof of his mouth. 'I can find a cure for this,' thought he. 'Now I will milk my cow and quench my thirst.'

So he tied her to the stump of a tree, and held his leathern cap to milk into, but not a drop was to be had. Who would have thought that this cow, which was to bring him milk and butter and cheese, was all that time utterly dry? Hans had not thought of looking to that.

While he was trying his luck in milking, and managing the matter very clumsily, the uneasy beast began to think him very troublesome, and at last gave him such a kick on the head as knocked him down. And there he lay senseless. Luckily a butcher soon came by, driving a pig in a wheelbarrow.

"What is the matter with you, my man?" said the butcher, as he helped him up. Hans told him what had happened, how he was dry and wanted to milk his cow, but found the cow was dry too.

Then the butcher gave him a flask of ale, saying, "There, drink and refresh yourself, your cow will give you no milk. Don't you see she is an old beast, good for nothing but the slaughterhouse?"

"Alas, alas!" said Hans. "Who would have thought it? What a shame to take my horse and give me only a dry cow! If I kill her, what will she be good for? I hate beef, it is not tender enough for me. If it were a pig now – like that fat gentleman you are driving along at his ease – one could do something with it. It would at any rate make some great sausages."

"Well," said the butcher, "I don't like to say no, when one is asked to do a neighbourly thing. To please you I will change, and give you my fine fat pig for the cow."

"Heaven reward you for your kindness and self-denial!" said Hans, as he gave the butcher the cow, and taking the pig off the wheelbarrow, drove it away, holding it by the string that was tied to its leg.

So on he jogged, and all seemed now to go right with him – he had met with some misfortunes, to be sure, but he was now well repaid for all. How could it be otherwise with such a travelling companion as he had at last got?

The next man he met was a countryman carrying a fine white goose. The countryman stopped to ask what was the time. This led to further chat, and Hans told him all his luck, how he had so many good bargains, and how all the world went gay and

smiling with him. The countryman then began to tell his tale, and said he was going to take the goose to a christening. "Feel," said he, "how heavy it is, and yet it is only eight weeks old. Whoever roasts it will find plenty of fat upon it, it has lived so well!"

"You're right," said Hans, "but if you talk of fat, my pig is no trifle."

The countryman began to look grave, and shook his head. "Listen!" said he. "My worthy friend, you seem a good sort of fellow, so I can't help doing you a kind turn. Your pig may get you into a scrape. In the village I just came from, the squire has had a pig stolen out of his sty. I was afraid when I saw you that you had got the squire's pig. If you have, and they catch you, it will be a bad job for you."

Hans in Luck

Poor Hans was frightened. "Good man," cried he, "I know nothing of where the pig was either bred or born, but he may have been the squire's for all I can tell – you know this country better than I do. Take my pig and give me the goose."

"I ought to have something into the bargain," said the countryman, "give a fat goose for a pig, indeed! 'Tis not everyone would do so much for you as that. However, I will not be hard upon you." Then he took the string in his hand, and drove off the pig by a side path, while Hans went on the way homewards free from care. 'After all,' thought he, 'that chap is pretty well taken in. I don't care whose pig it is, but wherever it came from it has been a very good friend to me. I have much the best of the bargain. First there will be a capital roast, then the fat will find me in goose grease for six months, and then there are all the white feathers. I will put them into my pillow, and then I shall sleep soundly. Talk of a pig, indeed! Give me a fine fat goose.'

As he came to the next village, he saw a scissor-grinder with his wheel, working and singing.

Hans stood looking on for a while, and at last said, "You must be well off, master grinder! You seem so happy at your work."

"Yes," said the other, "mine is a golden trade. A good grinder never puts his hand into his pocket without finding money in it – but where did you get that beautiful goose?"

"I did not buy it, I gave a pig for it."

"And where did you get the pig?"

"I gave a cow for it."

"And the cow?"

"I gave a horse for it."

"And the horse?"

"I gave a lump of silver as big as my head for it."

"And the silver?"

"Oh! I worked hard for that seven long years."

"You have done well in the world," said the grinder. "If you could find money in your own pocket whenever you put your hand in it, your fortune would be made."

"Very true – but how is that to be managed?"

"How? Why, you must turn grinder like myself. You only want a grindstone, the rest will come of itself. Here is one that is but little the worse for wear. I would not ask more than the value of your goose for it – will you buy?"

"How can you ask?" said Hans. "I should be the happiest man in the world, if I could have money whenever I put my hand in my pocket – what could I want more? There's the goose."

"Now," said the grinder, as he gave him a common rough stone that lay by his side, "this is a most capital stone, do but work it well enough, and you can make an old nail cut with it."

Hans took the stone, and went his way with a light heart. He said to himself, 'Surely I must have been born in a lucky hour, everything I could want or wish for comes of itself.'

In the meantime, Hans began to be tired and hungry, for he had given away his last penny. At last he could go no farther, for the stone tired him sadly, and he dragged himself to the side of a river, that he might take a drink of water, and rest a while. So he laid the stone by his side on the bank – but, as he stooped down to drink, he forgot it, pushed it a little, and down it rolled, plump into the stream.

He watched it sinking, then sprang up and danced for joy, and fell upon his knees and thanked heaven, with tears in his eyes, for its kindness in taking away his only plague, the ugly heavy stone.

"How happy am I!" cried he. "Nobody was ever so lucky as I." Then up he got with a light heart, free from all his troubles, and walked on till he reached his mother's house, and told her how very easy the road to good luck was.

The Wind and the Sun

By James Baldwin

The Wind and the Sun once had a dispute as to which was the stronger of the two.

"Do you see that traveller plodding along the road?" said the Wind. "Who can first strip him of his cloak will be the winner."

"Agreed," said the Sun.

The Wind began first. He blew a blast that sent leaves flying. He raised clouds of dust in the road, bent the tops of the trees to the ground and even tore up one oak by the roots. But the traveller drew his cloak tightly around him, and kept on his way.

Then the Sun began. He burst out from behind a cloud, and darted his beams upon the traveller. Soon the heat was so great that he stopped to wipe the sweat from his face.

"Ah!" he said. "It is so hot!" He threw off his cloak, and carried it under his arm. When he came to a tree by the roadside he sat down in its shade to cool himself.

After that, the Wind never claimed to be stronger than the Sun.

Straw, Coal and Bean

By the Brothers Grimm

*A*n old woman lived in a village. She had gathered a serving of beans and wanted to cook them, so she prepared a fire in her fireplace. To make it burn faster she lit it with a handful of straw. While she was pouring the beans into the pot, one of them fell unnoticed to the floor, coming to rest next to a piece of straw. Soon afterward a glowing coal jumped out of the fireplace and landed

next to them. The straw said, "Friends, where do you come from?"

The coal answered, "I jumped from the fireplace, to my good fortune. If I had not forced my way out, I surely would have died. I would have been burned to ash."

The bean said, "I too saved my skin. If the old woman had gotten me into the pot I would have been cooked to mush without mercy, just like my comrades."

"Would my fate have been any better?" said the straw. "The old woman sent all my brothers up in fire and smoke. She grabbed sixty at once and killed them. Fortunately I slipped through her fingers."

"What should we do now?" asked the coal.

"Because we have so fortunately escaped death," answered the bean, "I think that we should join together as comrades. To prevent some new misfortune from befalling us here, let us together make our way to another land."

Straw, Coal and Bean

This proposal pleased the other two, and they set forth all together.

They soon came to a small brook, and because there was neither a bridge nor a walkway there, they did not know how they would get across it.

Then the straw had a good idea, and said, "I will lay myself across it and you can walk across me like on a bridge."

So the straw stretched himself from one bank to the other. The coal, who was a hot-headed fellow, stepped brashly onto the newly constructed bridge, but when he got to the middle and heard the water rushing beneath him, he took fright, stopped, and did not dare to go any further. Then the straw caught fire, broke into two pieces, and fell into the brook. The coal slid after him, hissed as he fell into the water, and gave up the ghost.

The bean who had cautiously stayed behind on the bank had to laugh at the event. He could not stop, and he laughed so fiercely that he burst. Now he too would have died, but fortunately a wandering tailor was there, resting near the brook. Having a compassionate heart, he got out a needle and thread and sewed the bean back together.

The bean thanked him most kindly. However, because he had used black thread, since that time all beans have had a black seam.

Rosy's Journey

By Louisa May Alcott

Rosy was a little girl who lived with her mother in a small house in the woods. They were very poor, for the father had gone away to dig for gold, and had not come back. They had to work hard to get food to eat and clothes to wear. The mother spun yarn when she was able, for she was often sick, and Rosy did all she could to help. She milked the red cow and fed the hens, dug the garden, and went to town to sell the yarn and the eggs.

She was very good and sweet, and everyone loved

her, but the neighbours were all poor, and could do little to help the child. So, when at last the mother died, the cow and hens and house had to be sold to pay the doctor and the debts. Then Rosy was left all alone, with no mother, no home and no money to buy clothes or food.

"What will you do?" said the people, who were very sorry for her.

"I will go and find my father," answered Rosy.

"But he is far away, and you don't know just where he is, up among the mountains. Stay with us and spin on your little wheel, and we will buy the yarn and take care of you."

"No, I must go, for mother told me to, and my father will be glad to have me. I'm not afraid, for everyone is good to me," said Rosy, gratefully.

Then the people gave her a warm red cloak, and a basket with a little loaf and bottle of milk in it, and some pennies to buy more to eat when the bread was gone. They all kissed her, and wished her good luck, and she trotted away through the wood to find her father.

For some days she got on very well, for the woodcutters were kind, and let her sleep in their huts and gave her things to eat. But by and by she came to lonely places, where there were no houses and then she was afraid. At these times Rosy would climb up in the trees to sleep and had to eat berries and leaves.

She made a fire at night so wild beasts would not come near her, and if she met other travellers, she was so young and innocent no one had the heart to hurt her. She was kind to everything she met, so all little creatures were friends to her, as we shall see.

One day, as she was resting by a river, she saw a tiny fish on the bank, nearly dead for want of water.

"Poor thing! Go and be happy again," she said, softly taking him up, and dropping him into the cool river.

"Thank you, dear child. I'll not forget, but will

199

help you some day," said the fish, when he had taken a good drink, and felt better.

"Why, how can a tiny fish help such a great girl as I am?" laughed Rosy.

"Wait and see," answered the fish, as he swam away with a flap of his little tail.

Rosy went on her way, and forgot all about it. But she never forgot to be kind, and soon after, as she was looking in the grass for strawberries, she found a field mouse with a broken leg.

"Please help me! Take me to my nest, or my babies will starve," cried the poor little mouse.

"Yes, I will. Have some berries, so that you can rest till your leg is better, and still have food to eat."

Rosy took the mouse carefully in her little hand and tied up the broken leg with a leaf of spearmint and a blade of grass. Then she carried her to the nest under the roots of an old tree where four baby mice were squeaking sadly for their mother. She made a bed of thistledown for the sick mouse, and put close within reach all the berries and seeds she could find, and brought an acorn-cup of water from the spring, so they could be comfortable.

"Good Rosy, I shall pay you well for all this kindness some day," said the little mouse, when she was done.

"Thank you little mouse, but I'm afraid you might not be big enough to do very much," answered Rosy, sweetly, as she hurried off to continue on her journey.

"Wait and see," called the mouse, and all the little ones squeaked as if they said the same.

Some time after, as Rosy lay up in a tree, waiting for the sun to rise, she heard a great buzzing close by and saw a fly caught in a cobweb that went from one twig to another. A big spider was trying to spin him all up, and the poor fly was struggling to get away before his legs and wings were helpless.

Rosy put up her finger and pulled down the web, and the spider ran away at once to hide under the leaves. But the fly sat on Rosy's hand, cleaning his wings, and buzzing so loud for joy that it sounded like a little trumpet.

"You've saved my life, and I'll save yours, if I can," said the fly, twinkling his bright eye at Rosy.

"You silly thing, you can't help me," answered Rosy, climbing down, while the fly buzzed away, saying, like the mouse and fish, "Wait and see, wait and see."

Rosy trudged on and on, till at last she came to the sea. The mountains were on the other side, but how should she get over the wide water? No ships were there, and she had no money to hire one if there had been any, so she sat on the shore, very tired and sad, and cried a few big tears that were as salty as the sea.

"Hello!" called a bubbly sort of voice close by, and the fish popped up his head. Rosy ran to see him straightaway.

"I've come to help you," said the fish.

"How can you, when I need a ship, and someone to show me the way?" answered Rosy.

"I shall just call my friend the whale and he will take you over. He is far better than a ship because he knows these waters – you won't get wrecked with him. Don't you worry if he spouts and flounces about a good deal, he is only playing – so you needn't be frightened."

Down dived the little fish, and Rosy waited to see what would happen, for she didn't believe such a tiny thing could really bring a whale to help her cross the water.

Presently what looked like a small island came floating through the sea, and turning round, so that its tail touched the shore, the whale said, in a roaring voice that made her jump. "Come aboard, little girl, and hold on tight. I shall carry you wherever you like."

It was rather a slippery bridge, and Rosy was rather scared of this big, strange boat, but she got safely over, and held on fast. Then, with a roll and a plunge, off went the whale, spouting water, while his tail steered him like the rudder of a ship. Rosy liked it, and looked down into the deep sea, where all sorts of strange and lovely things were to be seen. Great fishes came and looked at her, dolphins played near to amuse her, the pretty nautilus sailed by in its transparent boat, and porpoises made her laugh with their rough play. Mermaids brought her pearls and red coral to wear, sea-apples to eat, and at night sung her to sleep with their sweet lullabies.

So she had a very pleasant voyage, and ran on shore with many thanks to the good whale, who gave a splendid spout and swam away.

Then Rosy travelled along till she came to a

desert. Hundreds of miles of hot, dry sand, with no trees or brooks or houses.

"I never can go that way," she said. "I should starve, and soon be worn out walking in that hot sand. What shall I do?"

"Quee, quee!
Wait and see.
You were good to me,
So here I come,
From my little home,
To help you willingly,"

said a friendly voice, and there was the mouse, looking at her with its bright eyes full of gratitude.

"Why, you dear little thing, I'm very glad to see you, but I'm sure you can't help me across this desert," said Rosy, stroking its soft back.

"That's easy enough," answered the mouse, rubbing its paws briskly. "I'll just call my friend the lion, he lives here, and he'll take you across."

"Oh, I'm afraid he'd rather eat me. How dare you call that fierce beast?" cried Rosy, much surprised.

"I gnawed him out of a net once, and he promised to help me. He is a noble animal and he will keep his word."

Then the mouse sang, in its shrill little voice:

"*O lion, grand,*
   Come over the sand,
   And help me now, I pray!
   Here's a little lass,
   Who wants to pass,
   Please carry her on her way."

In a moment a loud roar was heard, and a splendid yellow lion, with fiery eyes and a long mane, came bounding over the sand to meet them.

"What can I do for you, tiny friend?" he said, looking at the mouse, who was not a bit frightened, though Rosy hid behind a rock, expecting every moment to be eaten.

Mousie told him, and the good lion said pleasantly, "I'll take the child along. Come on, my dear, sit on my back and hold fast to my mane, for I'm swift, and you might fall off."

Then he crouched down like a great cat, and Rosy climbed up, for he was so kind she could not fear him, and away they went, racing over the sand till her hair whistled in the wind. As soon as she got her breath, she thought it great fun to go flying along, while other lions and tigers rolled their fierce eyes at her, but dared not touch her, for this lion was king of all, and she was quite safe.

They met a train of camels with loads on their backs, and the people travelling with them wondered what strange thing was riding that fine lion. It looked like a very large monkey in a red cloak, but went so fast they never saw that it was a little girl.

"How glad I am that I was kind to the mouse, for if the good little creature had not helped me, I never could have crossed this desert," said Rosy, as the lion walked awhile to rest himself.

"And if the little mouse had not gnawed me out of the net I never should have come at her call. You see, little people can conquer big ones, and make them gentle and friendly by kindness," answered the lion, wisely.

Then away they went again, faster than ever, till they came to the green country. Rosy thanked the good beast, and he ran back, for if anyone saw him, they would try to catch him.

'Now I have only to climb up these mountains and find father,' thought Rosy, as she saw the great hills before her, with many steep roads winding up to the top, and far, far away rose the smoke from the huts where the men lived and dug for gold.

She started off bravely, but took the wrong road, and after climbing a long while found the path blocked with rocks over which she could not climb.

Now Rosy was extremely tired and hungry, for all her food was gone, and there were no houses in this wild place. Night was coming on, and it was very cold. She was afraid she would freeze before morning, but dared not go on lest she should fall down some steep hole and be killed. Much discouraged, she lay down on the moss and cried a little, then she tried to sleep, but something kept buzzing in her ear, and looking carefully she saw a fly prancing about on the moss, as if anxious to make her listen to his song:

> *"Rosy, my dear,*
> *Don't cry – I'm here*
> *To help you all I can.*
> *I'm only a fly,*
> *But you'll see that I*
> *Will keep my word like a man."*

Rosy couldn't help laughing to hear the brisk
little fellow talk as if he could do great things, but
she was very glad to see him and hear his cheerful
song, so she held out her finger, and while he sat
there told him all her troubles.

"Bless your heart! My friend the eagle will carry
you right up the mountains and leave you at your
father's door," cried the fly, and he was off with a
flirt of his gauzy wings, for he meant what he said.

Rosy was not at all afraid after the whale and the
lion, so when a great eagle swooped down and
alighted near her, she just looked at his sharp claws,
big eyes, and crooked beak as coolly as if he had
been a cock-robin.

He liked her courage, and said kindly in his
rough voice, "Hop up, little girl, and sit among my
feathers. Hold me fast round the neck, or you may
grow dizzy and fall."

Rosy nestled down among the thick brown
feathers, and put both arms round his neck, and

whiz they went, up, up,
up, higher and
higher, till the
trees looked like
grass, they were
so far below.

At first it
was very cold,
and Rosy cuddled
deeper into her
feather bed, then, as
they came nearer to
the sun, it grew warm,
and she peeped out to see
the huts standing in a green spot
on the top of the mountain.

"Here we are. You'll find all the men are down in
the mine now. They won't come up till morning, so
you will have to wait for your father. Goodbye,
good luck, my dear." And the eagle soared away,

higher still, to his nest among the clouds.

It was night now, but fires were burning in all the houses, so Rosy went from hut to hut trying to find her father's, so that she might rest while she waited. At last in one the picture of a pretty little girl hung on the wall, and under it was written, 'My Rosy'. She knew that this was the right place so she ate some supper and went to bed.

While she slept a storm came on – thunder rolled and lightning flashed, the wind blew a gale and rain poured – but Rosy didn't wake till dawn, when she heard men shouting:

"Quick! Run, run! The river is rising!"

Rosy ran out to see what was the matter and the wind nearly blew her away. She soon found that the heavy rain had made the river overflow till it began to wash the banks away.

"What shall I do? What shall I do?" cried Rosy, watching the men rush about like ants, getting their bags of gold ready to carry off before the water swept them away, if it became a flood.

As if in answer to her cry, Rosy heard a voice:

"*Splash, dash!*
Rumble and crash!
Here come the beavers gay,
See what they do,
Rosy, for you,
Because you helped me one day."

And there in the water was the little fish swimming about, while an army of beavers began to pile up earth and stones in a high bank to keep the river back. How they worked, digging and heaping with teeth and claws, and beating the earth hard with their strange tails like shovels! Rosy and the men watched them work, glad to be safe, while the storm cleared up, and by the time the dam was made, all danger was over. Rosy looked into the faces of the rough men, hoping her father was there,

and was just going to ask one of them about him, when a great shouting rose up again, and everyone ran to the pit hole, shouting:

"The sand has fallen in! The poor fellows will be smothered! How can we get them out?"

Rosy ran too, feeling as if her heart would break, for her father was down in the mine and would die soon if air did not come to him. The men dug as hard as they could, but it was a long job and they feared they would not be in time.

Suddenly hundreds of moles came scampering along, and began to burrow down through the earth, making many holes for air to go in. They knew how to build galleries through the ground better than men can. Everyone was so surprised that they stopped to look on, for the dirt flew like rain as the busy little fellows scratched and dug.

"What does it mean?" said the men. "They work faster than we can, and better, but who sent them? Is this strange little girl a fairy?"

Before Rosy could speak, all heard a shrill, small voice singing:

"*They come at my call,*
  And though they are small,
  They'll dig the passage clear.
  I never forget,
  We'll save them yet,
  For love of Rosy dear."

Then all saw a little grey mouse sitting on a stone, waving her tail about and pointing with her tiny paw to show the moles where to dig.

The men laughed, and Rosy began to tell them who she was. Then all of a sudden a cry came from the pit, and they saw that the way was clear, so they could pull the buried men up. In a minute they got ropes and soon had ten poor fellows safe on the ground, pale and dirty. They were shouting loudly as if they were crazy:

"Tom's got it! Tom's got it! Hooray for Tom!"

"What is it?" cried the others, and then they saw Tom come up with the biggest lump of gold ever found in the mountains.

Everyone was glad of Tom's luck, for he was a good man, and had worked a long time, and been sick, and couldn't go back to his wife and child. When he saw Rosy, he dropped the lump, and caught her up in his arms, saying:

"My little girl! She's better than a million pounds of gold."

Then Rosy was very happy and went back to the hut. She had a lovely time telling her father all about her travels. He cried for a long time when he heard that her poor mother had died before she could have any of the good things the gold would buy them.

"We will go away and be happy together in the pleasantest home I can find, and never part any more, my darling," said the father, kissing Rosy as

217

she sat on his knee with her arms around his neck.

She was just going to say something very sweet to comfort him, when a fly landed on her arm and buzzed loudly:

> "*Don't drive me away,*
> *But hear what I say,*
> *Bad men want the gold,*
> *They will steal it tonight,*
> *And you must take flight,*
> *So be quiet and busy and bold.*"

"I was afraid someone would try to take my gold away. I'll pack up at once, and we will creep off while the other men are still busy at work. I'm afraid we can't travel fast enough to be safe if they miss us and come after," said Tom, while he bundled his lump of gold into a bag. He looked very sober, for some of the miners were wild fellows, and might kill him for his gold. But the fly sang again:

"Slip away with me,
And you will see
What a wise little thing am I,
For the road I show
No man can know,
Since it's up in the pathless sky."

Then they followed the fly to a quiet nook in the wood, and there were the eagle and his mate waiting to fly away with them so fast and so far that no one could follow. Rosy and the bag of gold were put on the mother eagle, Tom sat astride the king bird, and away they flew to a great city, where the little girl and her father lived happily together all their lives.

The Two Sisters

By Flora Annie Steel

*O*nce upon a time there were two sisters who were as like each other as two peas in a pod, but one was good, and the other was bad-tempered. Now their father had no work, so the girls began to think of going to be servants.

"I will go first and see what I can make of it," said the younger sister, ever so cheerfully, "then you, sis, can follow if I have good luck."

So she packed up a bundle, said goodbye, and started to find a place, but no one in the town wanted a girl, so she went farther afield into the country. And as she journeyed she came upon an oven in which a lot of loaves were baking.

Now as she passed, the loaves cried out with one voice, "Little girl! Little girl! Take us out! Please take us out! We have been baking for seven years, and no one has come to take us out. Do take us out or we shall soon be burned!"

Then, being a kind, obliging little girl, she stopped, put down her bundle, took out the bread, and went on her way, saying, "You will be more comfortable now."

After a time she came to a cow lowing beside an empty pail, and the cow said to her, "Little girl! Little girl! Milk me! Please milk me! Seven years have I been waiting, but no one has yet come to milk me!"

So the kind girl stopped, put down her bundle, milked the cow into the pail, and went on her way, saying, "Now you will be more comfortable."

By and by she came to an apple tree so laden with fruit that its branches were nigh to break, and the apple tree called to her:

"Little girl! Little girl! Please shake my branches. The fruit is so heavy I can't stand straight!"

Then the kind girl stopped, put down her bundle, and shook the branches so that the apples fell off, and the tree could stand straight. Then she went on her way, saying, "You will be more comfortable now."

So she journeyed on till she came to a house where an old witch lived. Now this witch wanted a maid, and promised good wages. Therefore the girl agreed to stop with her and try how she liked service. She had to sweep the floor, keep the house clean and tidy, the fire bright and cheery. But there was one thing the witch said she must never do, and that was look up the chimney.

"If you do," said the witch, "something will fall down on you, and you will come to a bad end."

Well, the girl swept and dusted and made up the fire, but never a penny of wages did she see.

Now the girl wanted to go home as she did not like witch service, for the witch used to have boiled babies for supper and bury the bones under some stones in the garden. But she did not like to go home penniless, so she stayed on, sweeping and dusting and doing her work, just as if she was pleased.

Then one day, as she was sweeping up the hearth, down tumbled some soot, and, without remembering she was forbidden to look up the chimney, she looked up to see where the soot came from. And, lo and behold – a big bag of gold fell plump into her lap.

Now the witch happened to be out on one of her witch errands, so the girl thought it a fine opportunity to be off home.

So she kilted up her petticoats and started to run home, but she had only gone a little way when she heard the witch coming after her on her broomstick. Now the apple tree she had helped happened to be quite close, so the girl ran up to it and cried,

"*Apple tree! Apple tree, hide me*
  So the old witch can't find me,
  For if she does she'll pick my bones,
  And bury me under the garden stones."

Then the apple tree said, "Of course I will. You helped me to stand straight, and one good turn deserves another."

So the apple tree hid her finely in its green branches, and when the witch flew past saying,

"*O Tree of mine! Tree of mine!*
  Have you seen my naughty little maid
  With a willy willy wag and a great big bag,
  She's stolen my money – all I had?"

The apple tree answered:

"No, Mother dear,
Not for seven year!"

So the witch flew on the wrong way, and the girl
got down, thanked the tree politely, and started
again. But just as she got to where the cow was
standing beside the pail, she heard the witch
coming again, so she ran to the cow and cried,

"Cow! Cow, please hide me
So the witch can't find me,
If she does she'll pick my bones,
And bury me under the garden stones!"

"Of course," said the cow.
"I owe you a favour."
So when the witch flew by
and called to the cow,

226

The Two Sisters

"O Cow of mine! Cow of mine!
Have you seen my naughty little maid
With a willy willy wag and a great big bag,
Who stole my money – all I had?"

The cow just said politely:

"No, Mother dear,
Not for seven year!"

Then the old witch went on in the wrong
direction, and the girl started fresh on her way
home, but just as she got to where the oven stood,
she heard the old witch coming behind her again,
so she ran as fast as she could to the oven and cried,

"O Oven! Oven! Hide me
So as the witch can't find me,
For if she does she'll pick my bones,
And bury them under the garden stones."

Then the oven said, "I am afraid there is no room
for you, as another batch of bread is baking, but
there is the baker – ask him."

So she asked the baker, and he said, "Of course I
will. You saved my last batch from being burned, so
run into the bakehouse, you will be quite safe there,
and I will settle the witch for you."

So she hid in the bakehouse, only just in time,
for there was the old witch calling angrily,

"O Man of mine! Man of mine!
  Have you seen my naughty little maid
  With a willy willy wag and a great big bag,
  Who's stole my money – all I had?"

Then the baker replied, "Look in the oven. She
may be there."

And the witch alighted from her broomstick and
peered into the oven, but she could see no one.

"Creep in and look in the farthest corner," said

the baker slyly, and the witch crept in. Bang! He shut the door in her face, and there she was roasting. And when she came out with the bread she was all crisp and brown, and had to go home as best she could and put cold cream all over her!

But the kind, obliging little girl got safely home with her bag of money.

Now the ill-tempered elder sister was very jealous of this good luck, and determined to get a bag of gold for herself. So she in her turn packed up a bundle and started to seek service by the same road. But when she came to the oven, and the loaves begged her to take them out because they had been baking seven years and were nigh to burning, she tossed her head and said, "A likely story indeed, that I should burn my fingers to save your crusts. No, thank you!"

And with that she went on till she came across the cow standing waiting to be milked beside the pail. But when the cow said, "Little girl! Little girl!

Milk me! Please milk me, I've waited seven years to be milked."

She only laughed and replied, "You can keep waiting! I'm not your dairymaid!"

And with that she went on till she came to the apple tree, all overburdened by its fruit. But when it begged her to shake its branches, she only giggled, and plucking one ripe apple, said, "One is enough for me, you can keep the rest yourself."

And with that she went on munching the apple, till she came to the witch's house.

Now the witch, though she had got over being crisp and brown from the oven, was angry with all little maids, and made up her mind this one should not trick her. For a long time she never left the house, thus the ill-tempered sister never had a chance of looking up the chimney, as she had meant to do. And she had to dust and clean and brush and sweep ever so hard, until she was quite tired out.

Until one day, when the witch went into the

garden to bury her bones, she seized the moment, looked up the chimney, and, sure enough, a bag of gold fell plump into her lap! Well! She was off with it in a moment, and ran and ran till she came to the apple tree, when she heard the witch behind her. So she cried as her sister had done,

> "*Apple tree! Apple tree, hide me*
> *So the old witch can't find me,*
> *For if she does she'll break my bones,*
> *Or bury me under the garden stones.*"

But the apple tree said, "No room here! I've too many apples." So she had to run on, and when the witch on her broomstick came flying by and called,

> "*O Tree of mine! Tree of mine!*
> *Have you seen a naughty little maid*
> *With a willy willy wag and a great big bag,*
> *Who's stolen my money – all I had?*"

The apple tree replied, "Yes, Mother dear, she's gone down there."

Then the witch went after her, caught her, gave her a thorough good beating, took the bag of money away from her, and sent her home without a penny payment for all her dusting, sweeping, brushing and cleaning.

I Wonder

By Kate Douglas Wiggin

*O*nce on a time there was a man who had three sons – Peter, Paul, and the least of all, whom they called Youngling. I can't say the man had anything more than these three sons, for he hadn't one penny to rub against another. He told the lads, over and over again, that they must go out into the world and try to earn their bread, for at home there was nothing to be looked for but starving to death.

Now nearby the man's cottage was the king's palace, and, you must know, just against the

windows a great oak had sprung up, which was so
stout and tall that it took away all the light. The
king had said he would give untold treasure to the
man who could fell the oak, but no one was man
enough for that, for as soon as one chip of the oak's
trunk flew off, two grew in its stead.

A well, too, the king desired, which was to hold
water for the whole year, for all his neighbours had
wells, but he hadn't any, and that he thought a
shame. So the king said he would give both money
and goods to anyone who could dig him such a well
as would hold water for a whole year round, but no
one could do it, for the palace lay high, high up on a
hill, and they could only dig a few inches before
they came upon rock.

But, as the king had set his heart on having these
two things done, he had it given out far and wide,
in all the churches of his dominion, that he who
could fell the oak in the king's courtyard, and get a
well that would hold water the whole year round,

should have the princess and half the kingdom.

Well! You may easily know there was many a
man who came to try his luck, but all their hacking
and hewing, all their digging and delving, were of
no avail. The oak grew taller and stouter at every
stroke, and the rock grew no softer.

So one day the three brothers thought they'd set
off and try, too, and their father hadn't a word
against it, for, even if they didn't get the princess
and half the kingdom, it might happen that they
would get a place somewhere with a good master,
and that was all he wanted. So when the brothers
said they thought of going to the palace, their
father said "Yes" at once, and Peter, Paul and
Youngling went off from their home.

They had not gone far before they came to a fir
wood, and up along one side of it rose a steep
hillside, and as they went they heard something
hewing and hacking up on the hill among the trees.

"I wonder now what it is that is hewing away up

yonder?" said Youngling.

"You are always so clever with your wonderings," said Peter and Paul, both at once. "What wonder is it, pray, that a woodcutter should stand and hack up on a hillside?"

"Still, I'd like to see what it is, after all," said Youngling, and up he went.

"Oh, if you're such a child, it'll do you good to go and take a lesson," cried out his brothers after him.

But Youngling didn't care for what they said. He climbed the steep hillside towards where the noise came from, and when he reached the place, what do you think he saw?

Why, an axe that stood there hacking and hewing, all by itself, at the trunk of a fir tree.

"Good day," said Youngling. "So you stand here all alone and hew, do you?"

"Yes, here I've stood and hewed and hacked a long time, waiting for you, my lad," said the axe.

"Well, here I am at last," said Youngling, as he took the axe, pulled it off its haft, and stuffed both head and haft into his wallet.

So when he climbed down again to his brothers, they began to jeer and laugh at him.

"And now, what funny thing was it you saw up on the hillside?" they said.

"Oh, it was only an axe we heard," said Youngling.

When they had gone a bit farther they heard something digging and shovelling.

"I wonder," said Youngling, "what it is digging and shovelling up yonder at the top of the rock?"

"Ah, you're always so clever with your wonderings," said Peter and Paul again, "as if you'd never heard a woodpecker hacking and pecking at a hollow tree."

"Well, well," said Youngling, "I think it would be a piece of fun just to see what it really is."

And so off he set to climb the rock, while the others laughed and made fun of him. But he didn't care a bit for that. Up he clambered, and when he got near the top, what do you think he saw? Why, a spade that stood there digging and delving.

"Good day," said Youngling. "So you stand here all alone, and dig and delve?"

"Yes, that's what I do," said the spade, "and that's what I've done this many a long day, waiting for you, my lad."

"Well, here I am," said Youngling again, as he took the spade and knocked off its handle, and put it into his wallet, and then he climbed down again to his brothers.

"Well, what was it, so strange and rare," said

Peter and Paul, "that you saw up there at the top of the rock?"

"Oh," said Youngling, "nothing more than a spade. That was what we heard."

So they went on again a good bit, till they came to a brook. They were thirsty after their long walk, and so they sat beside the brook to have a drink.

"I have a great fancy to see where this brook comes from," said Youngling.

So up alongside the brook he went, in spite of all that his brothers shouted after

him. Nothing could stop him. On he went. And as he went up and up, the brook grew smaller and smaller, and at last, a little way farther on, what do you think he saw? Why, a great walnut, and out of that the water trickled.

"Good day," said Youngling again. "So you lie here and trickle, and run down all alone?"

"Yes," said the walnut, "and here have I trickled and run many a long day, waiting for you, my lad."

"Well, here I am," said Youngling, as he took a lump of moss and plugged up the hole, so that the water wouldn't run out. Then he put the walnut into his wallet, and ran down to his brothers.

"Well," said Peter and Paul, "have you found where the water comes from? A rare sight it must have been!"

"Oh, after all, it was only a hole it ran out of," said Youngling, and the others laughed and made game of him again, but Youngling didn't mind that a bit.

So when the brothers had gone a little farther, they came to the king's palace. But as every man in the kingdom had heard that he might win the princess and half the realm, if he could fell the big oak and dig the king's well, so many had come to try their luck that the oak was now twice as stout and big as it had been at first, for you will remember that two chips grew for every one they hewed out with their axes.

So the king had now laid it down as a punishment that if anyone tried and couldn't fell the oak, he should be put on a barren island, and both his ears were to be clipped off. But the two brothers didn't let themselves be frightened by this threat, they were quite sure they could fell the oak, and Peter, as he was the eldest, was to try his hand first, but it went with him as with all the rest who had hewn at the oak – for every chip he cut two grew in its place. So the king's men seized him, and clipped off his ears, and put him out on the island.

Now Paul was to try his luck, but he fared just the same. When he had hewn two or three strokes, they began to see the oak grow, and so the king's men seized him, too, and clipped his ears, and put him out on the island, and they clipped his ears closer, because they said he ought to have taken a lesson from his brother.

So now Youngling was to try.

"If you want to look like a marked sheep, we're quite ready to clip your ears at once, and then you'll save yourself some trouble," said the king, for he was angry with him for his brothers' sake.

"Well, I'd just like to try first," said Youngling, and so he was given permission. Then he took his axe out of his wallet and fitted it to its handle.

"Hew away!" said he to his axe, and away it hewed, making the chips fly again, so that it wasn't long before down came the oak.

When that was done, Youngling pulled out his spade and fitted it to its handle.

"Dig away!" said he to his spade, and so the spade began to dig and delve till the earth and rock flew out in splinters, and he soon had the well deep enough, you may believe. And when he had got it as big and deep as he chose, Youngling took out his walnut and laid it in one corner of the well, and pulled the plug of moss out.

"Trickle and run," said Youngling, and so the nut trickled and ran till the water gushed out of the hole in a stream, and soon the well was full.

So as Youngling had felled the oak that shaded the king's palace, and dug a well in the palace yard, he got the princess and half the kingdom, as the king had said, but it was lucky for Peter and Paul that they had lost their ears, else they might have grown tired of hearing how everyone said each hour of the day, "Well, after all, Youngling wasn't so much out of his mind when he took to wondering."

WHAT NONSENSE!

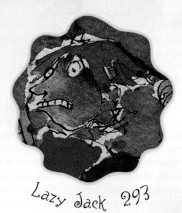

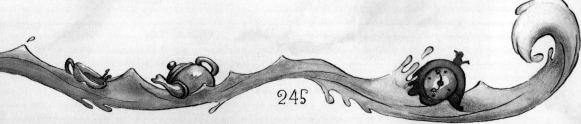

The Haughty Princess

By Patrick Kennedy

There was once a very worthy king, whose daughter was the greatest beauty that could be seen far or near. But she was as proud as Lucifer, and no king or prince would she agree to marry. Her father was tired out, and invited every king, and prince, and duke, and earl that he knew or didn't know to come to his court to give her one more trial. They all came, and the next day they

The Haughty Princess

stood in a row on the lawn, and the princess walked along in front of them to make her choice. One was fat, and said she, "I won't have you, beer-barrel!" One was tall and thin, and to him she said, "I won't have you, ramrod!" To a white-faced man she said, "I won't have you, pale death!" and to a red-cheeked man she said, "I won't have you, cockscomb!"

She stopped a little before the last of all, for he was a fine man in face and form. She wanted to find some defect in him, but he had nothing remarkable but a ring of brown curling hair under his chin. She admired him for a short time, and then said, "I won't have you, whiskers!"

So all went away, and the king was so vexed he said to her, "Now to punish your impudence, I'll give you to the first beggar man or singing sthronshuch (lazy thing) that calls." And, sure enough, a fellow in rags, and hair that came to his shoulders, and a bushy red beard all over his face, came next morning and began to sing before the parlour window.

When the song was over the hall door was opened, the singer asked in, the priest brought, and the princess married to Beardy. She roared and she bawled, but her father didn't mind her. "There," said he to the bridegroom," is five guineas for you. Take your wife out of my sight, and never let me lay eyes on you or her again."

Off he led her, and dismal enough she was. The only thing that gave her relief was the tones of her husband's voice and his genteel manners.

"Whose wood is this?" said she, as they were going through one.

"It belongs to the king you called whiskers yesterday." He gave her the same answer about meadows and cornfields, and at last a fine city.

"Ah, what a fool I was!" said she to herself. "He was a fine man, and I might have had him for a husband." At last they were coming up to a poor cabin. "Why are you bringing me here?" said the poor lady.

"This was my house," said he, "and now it's yours." She began to cry, but she was tired and hungry, and went in with him. There was neither a table laid out, nor a fire burning, and she was obliged to help her husband to light it, and boil their dinner, and clean up the place after, and the next day he made her put on a stuff gown and a cotton handkerchief. When she had her house cleaned up, and no business to keep her employed, he brought home willows, peeled them, and showed her how to make baskets. But the hard twigs bruised her delicate fingers, and she began to cry. Well, then he asked her to mend their clothes, but the needle drew blood from her fingers, and she cried again.

He couldn't bear to see her tears, so he bought a boxful of earthenware pots, and sent her to the market to sell them. This was the hardest trial of all, but she looked so handsome and sorrowful, and had such a nice air about her, that all her pots and jugs and plates and dishes were gone before noon.

Well, her husband was so glad, he sent her with another box the next day. But her luck was deserting her. A drunken huntsman came riding up, and his beast got in among her ware, and broke them all. She went home crying, and her husband wasn't at all pleased. "I see," said he, "you're not fit for business. Come along, I'll get you a kitchen maid's place in the palace. I know the cook."

So the poor thing was obliged to stifle her pride

once more. She was kept very busy, and she went home to her husband every night, carrying her payment of scraps of leftover food wrapped in papers in her side pockets.

A week after she got the job there was great bustle in the kitchen. The king was going to be married, but no one knew who the bride was to be. Well, in the evening the cook filled the princess's pockets with cold meat and puddings, and then, said she, "Before you go, let us have a look at the great doings in the big parlour."

So they came near the door to get a peep, and who should come out but the king himself, as handsome as you please, and he was no other but King Whiskers himself.

"Your handsome helper must pay for her peeping," said he to the cook, when he spotted them, "and dance a jig with me."

Whether the princess would or not, he held her hand and brought her into the parlour. The fiddlers struck up, and away went him with her. But they hadn't danced two steps when the meat and the puddings flew out of her pockets. Everyone roared with laughter, and she flew to the door, crying piteously. But she was soon caught by the king, and taken into the back parlour.

"Don't you know me, my darling?" said he. "I'm King Whiskers, your husband the ballad singer, and the drunken huntsman. Your father knew me well enough when he gave you to me, and all was to drive your pride out of you."

Well, she didn't know how she was with fright and shame and joy. Love was uppermost anyhow, for she laid her head on her husband's breast and cried like a child.

The maids-of-honour soon had her away and dressed her as fine as hands and pins could do it, and there were her mother and father, too, and while the company were wondering what end of the handsome girl and the king, he and his queen, who

252

they didn't know in her fine clothes, and the other king and queen, came in, and such rejoicings and fine doings as there were, none of us will ever see!

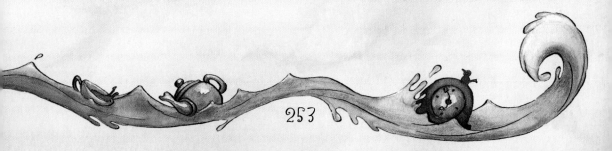

Nasreddin Hodja and the Smell of Soup

Anon

Nasreddin Hodja is what you might call a wise fool. He comes up with answers other people would never have thought of! He is a popular figure in Turkish folklore and there are many tales about him.

A beggar was walking along the road of the main market. He had begged a small piece of bread for himself, dry and old, and

Nasreddin Hodja and
the Smell of Soup

that was all he had to eat that day. Hoping to
get something to put on it, he went to a
nearby restaurant and begged for a small
portion of food, but was ordered out of
the inn empty handed. As he walked
out he stopped to stare at the rich
people enjoying the bowls of good
savoury soup. He lent over one of
the cauldrons that bubbled and
hissed on the charcoal fire and
took a deep breath to savour
its good smell, then turned
sadly to go. At that moment
the innkeeper came out and
seized his arm.

"Not so fast! You haven't
paid!" he exclaimed.

"Payment? But I have
had nothing," stammered
the confused beggar, "I

was only enjoying the smell of your soup."

"Then you must pay for the smell," insisted the innkeeper. "Do you think I cook my soup for a beggar to steal a smell from? I saw you take it."

The poor beggar had no money to pay, of course, so the innkeeper dragged him off to the Nasreddin Hodja, the judge. Hodja listened to the case most carefully, considering both the innkeeper's angry exclamations, and the beggar's protests that he had taken nothing.

"And you say you have no money?" he asked the poor man.

"Not a penny," stammered the terrified beggar.

Then Hodja turned to the innkeeper.

"So you insist on being paid for the smell?" he enquired.

"Indeed I do," said the innkeeper.

"Then I myself will pay you," said Hodja.

He drew some coins out of his pocket, and beckoned the innkeeper closer. The man went eagerly forward.

Hodja held the coins in his hands up to the innkeeper's ear and shook his hand gently so the coins rang together.

"You may go," he said.

The innkeeper said angrily, "But my payment..."

"This man took the smell of the soup," said Hodja, "and you have been paid with the sound of the money. Now go on your way."

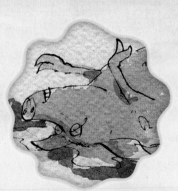

The Husband who was to Mind the House

By Peter Christen Asbjørnsen

Once upon a time there was a man who was so bad tempered and cross that he never thought his wife did anything right in the house. One evening, in hay-making time, he came home, scolding and shouting, and showing his teeth and making a commotion.

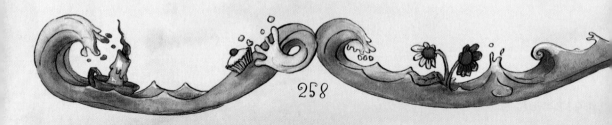

The Husband who was to Mind the House

"Dear love, don't be so angry, that's a good man," said his patient wife. "Tomorrow let's change jobs. I'll go out with the mowers and mow, and you can mind the house at home. We will swap chores, and see how we get on."

Yes, the husband thought that would do very well. He was quite willing, he said.

So early the next morning, his wife took a scythe over her neck, and went out into the hay field with the mowers and began to mow, but the man was to mind the house, and do the work at home.

First of all he wanted to churn the butter, but when he had churned awhile, he got thirsty, and went down to the cellar to tap a barrel of ale.

After he had finished his drink he knocked in the bung. The husband was just putting in the tap when he heard a noise coming from the kitchen above. It was the pig! As fast as he could, he ran up the cellar steps, with the tap in his hand, to keep the pig from upsetting the churn, but when he got there, the pig

had knocked the churn over, and was rolling and grunting in the cream that was all over the floor.

He got so angry that he quite forgot the ale barrel, and ran at the pig as hard as he could. He caught it, too, just as it ran out of doors, and gave it such a powerful kick that he killed it on the spot. Then he remembered

The Husband who was to Mind the House

he had the tap in his hand, but when he got down
to the cellar, all the ale had run out of the barrel.

Then he went into the milk shed and found
enough cream left to fill the churn again, and so he
began to churn, for they had to have butter at
dinner. When he had churned a bit, he remembered
that their cow was still shut up in the barn, and
hadn't had a bit to eat or a drop to drink all
morning, although the sun was high. It occurred to
him that it was too far to take her down to the
meadow, so he'd just get her up on the roof, for it
was a sod roof, and a fine crop of grass was growing
there. The house was close against a steep hill, and
he thought if he laid a plank across to the back of
the roof he'd easily get the cow up.

But he couldn't leave the churn, for his little
baby was crawling about on the floor. 'If I leave it,'
he thought, 'the child will tip it over.' So he took the
churn on his back and went out with it, but then he
thought he'd better first draw water for the cow

before he put her on the roof. So he picked up a bucket to draw water out of the well, but, as he stooped over the edge of the well, all the cream ran out of the churn over his shoulder and down into the well.

Now it was near dinner time, and he hadn't even got the butter yet, so he thought he'd best boil the porridge, and filled the pot with water and hung it over the fire. When he had done that, it occurred to him that the cow might fall off the roof and break her legs or neck. So he climbed up on the house to tie her up. He tied one end of the rope to the cow's neck. He slipped the other end down the chimney and tied it around his own leg. Then he had to hurry, for the water was now boiling in the pot, and he had still to grind the oatmeal.

He began to grind away, but while he was hard at it, the cow fell off the roof, dragging the man up the chimney by the rope. There he stuck fast, and as for the cow, she hung halfway down the wall, swinging

between heaven and earth, for she could neither get down nor up.

Now the wife waited seven lengths and seven breadths for her husband to come and call her home to dinner, but he never came. At last she thought she'd waited long enough, and went home. But when she got home and saw the cow hanging there, she ran up and cut the rope with her scythe. When she did this, her husband fell down from within the chimney. When the old woman came inside, she found him upside down with his head in the porridge pot.

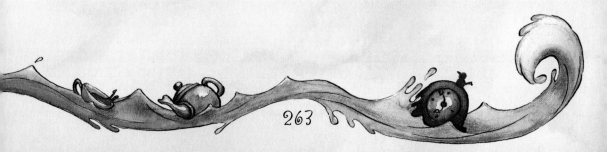

Nasreddin Hodja and the Pot

Anon

Nasreddin Hodja went to his neighbour to borrow a large cooking pot for a few days. When he returned it, the neighbour was surprised to find a smaller pot inside.

"What's this, Nasreddin?" he said

"Oh, your pot gave birth while in my house," Nasreddin replied, "and naturally as the larger pot is yours, so the smaller pot belongs to you also so I

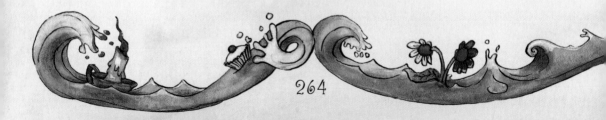

have brought it to you."

'What a fool!' thought the man, but he smiled and accepted the pot, pleased at his good fortune.

Some days later, Nasreddin asked if he might borrow the pot again. After a few weeks, the neighbour went to Nasreddin's house to ask for it back.

"Oh, I am sorry to tell you," said Nasreddin, "but your pot has died."

"Don't be so foolish" said the neighbour angrily. "Cooking pots don't die!"

"Are you sure?" said Nasreddin. "You didn't seem surprised when you heard it had given birth."

Sir Gammer Vans

By Joseph Jacobs

*L*ast Sunday morning at six o'clock in the
evening as I was sailing over the tops of the
mountains in my little boat, I met two men on
horseback riding on one mare. So I asked them,
could they tell me whether the little old woman was
dead yet who was hanged last Saturday week for
drowning herself in a shower of feathers?

They said they could not positively inform me,
but if I went to Sir Gammer Vans he could tell
me all about it.

Sir Gammer Vans

"But how am I to know the house?" said I.

"Ho, 'tis easy enough," said they, "for 'tis a brick house, built entirely of flints, standing alone by itself in the middle of sixty or seventy others just like it."

"Oh, nothing in the world is easier," said I.

"Nothing can be easier," said they. So I went on my way.

Now this Sir Gammer Vans was a giant, and a bottle-maker. And as all giants who are bottle-makers usually pop out of a little thumb-bottle from behind the door, so did Sir Gammer Vans.

"How d'ye do?" said he.

"Very well, I thank you," said I.

"Have some breakfast with me?"

"With all my heart," said I.

So he gave me a slice of beer, and a cup of cold veal. And there was a little dog under the table that picked up all the crumbs.

"Hang him," says I.

"No, don't hang him," said he, "for he killed a hare yesterday. And if you don't believe me, I'll show you the hare alive in a basket."

So he took me into his garden to show me the curiosities. In one corner there was a fox hatching eagle's eggs. In another there was an iron apple tree, entirely covered with pears and lead. In the third there was the hare that the dog killed yesterday alive in the basket.

Then he took me into the park to show me his deer. And I remembered that I had a warrant in my pocket to shoot venison for his majesty's dinner. So I set fire to my bow, poised my arrow, and shot amongst them. I broke seventeen ribs on one side, and twenty-one and a half on the other, but my arrow passed clean through without ever touching it, and the worst was I lost my arrow. However, I found it again in the hollow of a tree. I felt it. It felt clammy. I smelt it. It smelt of honey.

"Oh, ho," said I. "Here's a bee's nest," when out sprang a flight of partridges. I shot at them. Some say I killed eighteen, but I am sure I killed thirty-six, besides a dead salmon that was flying over the bridge, out of which I made an apple pie.

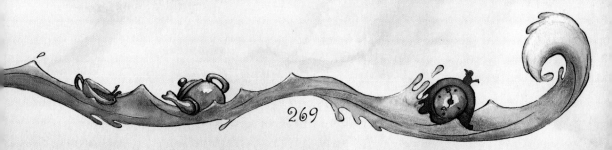

Carrie's Three Wishes

By Lucretia P Hale

People have to take great care with wishes – it is so easy to get them wrong. In this story, Carrie is an American girl living in the 19th century. She is certain she has thought of good wishes, but they still cause her a lot of trouble. The chariot she thinks of wishing for is not like a Roman chariot – it is a light carriage pulled by four horses.

Carrie Fraser was a great trouble to her mother, because she was always wishing for something she had not got.

Carrie's Three Wishes

"The other girls always have things that I don't," she complained to her mother. Her mother tried to explain to Carrie that she had a great many things the other girls didn't have.

"But they are not always wishing for my things, just as I wish for theirs."

"That is because they are not such 'teasers' as you are," her mother would reply.

One day, as usual, she had been complaining, and wishing she could have everything she wanted. Her mother said to her, "Do you remember the old story of the old couple who had their three wishes granted, and how they never got any good from it?"

"But that was because they acted like such geese," exclaimed Carrie. "I could never have been so elephantinely idiotic! First of all, they wasted one wish. They asked for a common, everyday sausage to come down the chimney, then they got into a stupid fight, and wished the sausage would settle on one of their noses, and then they had to waste their very last wish, by wishing it off again! It is too bad to have such luck come to such out-and-out idiots."

Mrs Fraser was just setting out for the village street, to order dinner. The governor was expected to pass through, and was to be met at the town hall. Jimmy, the only son in the family, had gone to see the show.

"Now, if he were a real, genuine governor," said Carrie, "like a prince in a fairytale, you would go and beseech him to grant your wishes. You would fall on your knees, or something, and he would beg you to rise, and your lovely daughter should have all that she wished."

"I am afraid you are very foolish," sighed Mrs Fraser, "but I will see the governor. Perhaps he can advise what is best."

It seemed to Carrie as if her mother were gone a great while. "She might have got six dinners!" she exclaimed to herself. "How tiresome! I wish I had gone down myself, anyway. All the girls and boys

272

have gone, and I might have seen the governor."

But she passed the time in rocking backwards and forwards in a rocking chair, for when the other girls had gone down town, and had urged her to go with them, she had been too lazy to go for her hat.

"If I had only a chariot and four (that means horses) to go down town with, and somebody to dress me and find my boots and my hat and my gloves, then it would have been worthwhile to go. I mean to write down a list of all my wishes, just in case there is somebody who should grant me the power to have them all."

And so she took out a little book from her pocket

and began to write down her wishes, as follows:

1. A chariot and four, man to drive, etc.
2. Maid to find and put on hat, boots, etc.
3. Plenty of hats, boots, and gloves for the maid to put on, and so that they could be found when wanted.

"If I had gloves in every drawer and on every shelf, I should not have to be looking for them. I might have a hat on every peg in the house except what Jimmy uses. I might have a sack over the back of every chair, and gloves in the pockets of each. The boots could be in each corner of the room and on all the top shelves. Let's see. That makes three wishes. They generally have three. If I strike out the maid, I can think of something else. Suppose I say something to eat, then. Chocolate creams! I never had enough yet."

At this moment Mrs Fraser returned, looking quite heated and breathless. She had to fling herself into a chair by the window to recover strength

enough to speak, and then her words came out in gasps. Carrie left her rocking chair and tried fanning her mother, for she saw she had something to say.

"What is it? What have you seen? Have you got something for me? Is the governor coming here? Couldn't you raise any dinner?"

"Yes, I saw him, I managed to see him," she gasped out. "The guns were firing, the cannon were booming, the bells were ringing."

"Oh! I dare say! I dare say!" cried Carrie, eager to hear more. "I could hear them up here. That was not worth going to town for. What did the governor say?"

"My dear! My dear!" panted Mrs Fraser, "he said you could have your three wishes."

"What! The chariot and four, the maid, and, no, the maid was scratched out, not the chocolates?" asked Carrie, in wonder.

"No, no! I don't know what you mean!" said

Mrs Fraser, "but you can have three wishes, and I have hurried home, for they are to be told as the clock strikes twelve – one today, one tomorrow, one the next day – the moment the clock strikes, and I am only just in time. You are to wish, and you will have just what you wish."

Both Carrie and her mother looked at the clock. The hand was just approaching twelve. Carrie could hear a little 'click' that always came from inside the clock before it struck.

"I have written out my wishes," she hurried to say, "but I don't want the chariot yet, because everybody is coming back from town. And I don't want any more hats and boots just now. But, oh! I do want some chocolate creams, and I wish this room was 'chock full' of them."

As she spoke the clock struck, and when it stopped she could speak no more, for the room was as full of chocolate creams as it could hold. They came rattling down upon her head, filling in all the

crannies of the room. They crowded into her half-open mouth, they filled her clutching hands. Luckily, Mrs Fraser was sitting near the open window, and the chocolate creams pushed her forward upon the sill. There were two windows. One was made of glass doors that were shut, the other, fortunately, was quite low, and Mrs Fraser seated herself on the edge, and succeeded in passing her feet over to the other side, a torrent of chocolate creams following her as she came. She then turned to see if she could help Carrie. Carrie was trying to eat her way toward the window, and stretched out her arms to her mother, who seized her, and with all her strength pulled her through the window.

"They are bully!" exclaimed Carrie, as soon as she was free. "They are the freshest I ever ate. Golumptious!"

"Oh, Carrie," said her mother, mournfully, "how can you use such expressions now, when you have wasted your brilliant opportunity on such an extravagant wish?"

"What! A whole roomful of chocolate creams do you consider a waste?" exclaimed Carrie. "Why, we shall be envied by all our neighbours, and, Mamma, you have been sighing over our expenses. Do you not see that we can make our fortune with chocolate creams? First, let us eat all we want before telling anybody, then let us give some to choice friends, and we will sell the rest."

All the time she was talking Carrie was putting in her hand for chocolate creams and cramming one after another. Mrs Fraser, too, did not refuse to taste them. How could they ever get into the parlour again, unless they were eaten up?

"I am sure that we can make quite a fortune," Carrie went on. "As soon as Jimmy comes home we can calculate how much it will be worth. The last time I was in Boston I gave fifteen cents for a quarter of a pound, and there were just thirteen chocolate creams. Now, you see. In my two hands I

can hold fourteen, now, how many times that do you suppose there are in the room?"

Mrs Fraser could not think. Carrie was triumphant.

"Jimmy will know how to calculate, for he knows how many feet and inches there are in the room. If not, he can measure, and we can row the chocolate creams out, and see how many go to a foot, and then we can easily find out. Of course, we shall sell them cheaper than they do in Boston, and so there will be a rush for them. It will be bully!"

"I am glad we happened to take this rocking chair out on the piazza this morning," said Mrs Fraser, languidly seating herself. "I don't see how we shall ever get into the parlour again."

"Jimmy and I will eat our way in fast enough," said Carrie, laughing, and Jimmy at that moment appeared with two friends, whom he had brought home to dinner.

They were all delighted when they understood

the situation, and had soon eaten a little place by
the window, inside the room.

"I quite forgot to buy any dinner," exclaimed
Mrs Fraser, starting up. "I meant to have ordered
a leg of mutton as I went down, and now it is too
late, and eggs for a pudding. Jimmy will have to
go down."

"Oh, the chocolate creams will do!" exclaimed
Carrie. "Don't you see, there's our first saving, and
my wish does not turn out so extravagant, after all.
The boys will be glad to have chocolate creams for
dinner, I'm sure."

The boys all said they would, as far as they could,
when their mouths were so full.

"We must put out an advertisement," said Carrie,
at last, as soon as she could stop to speak,
"'Chocolate creams sold cheap!' We may as well
make all we can. Suppose we look up some boxes
and baskets, Jimmy, to sell them in, and you boys
can go to the gate and tell people there are

chocolate creams for sale."

But all the boxes and baskets were soon filled, and only a little space made in the room. Jimmy pulled out the other rocking chair that Carrie had been sitting in, and she rested herself for a while.

"I declare, I never thought before I could eat enough chocolate creams, but they are a trifle sickening."

"My dear," said Mrs Fraser, "if you had not said 'chock full,' if you had said 'a great many,' or 'a trunkful,' or something of that sort."

"But I meant 'chock full,'" insisted Carrie. "I did not mean quite up to the ceiling. I didn't suppose that was what 'chock' meant. Now we know."

A great shouting was heard. All the boys of the town were gathering, and quite a crowd of people seemed coming near.

Mrs Fraser was a widow, and there was no man in the house. Jimmy was the nearest approach to a man that she could depend upon, and here he was,

leading a band of boys! She sent one of the boys she knew the best for Mr Stetson, the neighbouring policeman, who came quickly, having already seen the crowd of boys flocking to the house.

Carrie was trying to sell off her boxes for fifteen, ten, even five cents, but the crowd could not be easily appeased, for the boys could see across the windows the chocolate creams closely packed. "The room is chock full!" they exclaimed.

Mr Stetson examined the premises. "You'll find it hard work to get them chocolates out in a week, even if you set all the boys on them. I'd advise letting them in one by one to fill their pockets, each to pay a cent."

Even Carrie assented to this, and a line was formed, and boys let in through the window. They ate a way to the door that led into the entry, so that it could be opened and the room could be entered that way.

The boys now went in at the window and came

out at the door, eating as they went and filling their pockets. Carrie could not but sigh at thought of the Boston chocolates, more than a cent apiece! But the boys ate, and then the girls came and ate, but with night all had to leave, at last. It was possible to shut the window and lock it, and shut the door for the night, after they had gone.

"I don't see why the chocolates should not stay on there weeks and weeks," said Carrie to her mother. "Of course, they won't be so fresh, day after day, but they will be fresher than some in the shops. I'm awfully tired of eating them now, and feel as if I never want to see a chocolate cream again, but I suppose I shall feel different after a night's sleep, and I think Mr Stetson is wrong in advising us to sell them so low."

Mrs Fraser suggested she should like to go in the parlour to sit.

"But tomorrow is the day of the picnic," said Carrie, "and we shall be outdoors anyhow. I will take chocolate creams for my share. But, dear me! My dress is on the sofa – my best dress."

"I told you, my dear, one of the last things, to take it upstairs," said Mrs Fraser.

"And there it is, in the furthest corner of the room," exclaimed Carrie, "with all those chocolates scrouching on it. I'll tell you. I'll get Ben Sykes in early. He eats faster than any of the other boys, and he shall eat up toward my dress. He made a great hole in the chocolates this afternoon. I will have him come in early, and we don't go to the picnic till after twelve o'clock."

"And at twelve o'clock you have your second wish," said Mrs Fraser.

"Yes, Mamma," said Carrie, "and I have already decided what it shall be – a chariot and four. It will come just in time to take me to the picnic."

"Oh, my dear Carrie," said her mother, "do think what you are planning! Where would you keep your chariot and the four horses?"

"Oh! There will be a man to take care of them," said Carrie, "but I will think about it all night carefully."

At that very moment she went to sleep.

The next morning early, Carrie was downstairs. She found she could eat a few more chocolate creams, and Jimmy was in the same condition. She

proposed to him her plan of keeping the chocolates still for sale, but eating a way to the sofa in the corner, to her best dress.

Ben Sykes came early, and a few of the other boys. The rest were kept at home, because it turned out they had eaten too many and their parents would not let them come.

A good many of the older people came with baskets and boxes, and bought some to carry away, they were so delicious and fresh.

Meanwhile Ben Sykes was eating his way toward the corner. It was very hard making any passage, for as fast as he ate out a place others came tumbling in from the top. Carrie and Jimmy invented 'a kind of a tunnel' of chairs and ironing boards, to keep open the passage, and other boys helped eat, as they were not expected to pay.

But the morning passed quickly on. Mrs Fraser tried her best to persuade Carrie to wear another dress but she had set her mind on this one. She had a broad blue sash to wear with it, and the sash would not go with any other dress.

She watched the clock, she watched Ben, she went in under the ironing boards, to help him eat, although she had begun to loathe the taste of the chocolate creams.

Ben was splendid. He seemed to enjoy more the more he ate. Carrie watched him, as he licked them and ate with glowing eyes.

"Oh, Ben," Carrie suddenly exclaimed, "you can't seem to eat them fast enough. I wish your throat was as long as this room."

At this moment the clock was striking.

Carrie was ready to scream out her second wish, but she felt herself pushed in a strange way. Ben was on all fours in front of her, and now he pushed her back, back. His neck was so long that while his head was still among the chocolates, at the far corner of the room, his feet were now out of the door.

Carrie stood speechless. She had lost her wish by

her foolish exclamation. The faithful Ben, meanwhile, was flinging something through the opening. It was her dress, and she hurried away to put it on.

When she came down, everybody was looking at Ben. At first he enjoyed his long neck very much. He could stand on the doorstep and put his head far out up in the cherry trees and nip off cherries, which pleased both the boys and himself.

Instead of a chariot and four, Carrie went off in an open wagon, with the rest of the girls. It made her feel so to see Ben, with his long neck, that she got her mother's permission to spend the night with the friend in whose grounds the picnic was to be held.

She carried baskets of chocolate creams, and she found numbers of the girls, who had not eaten any, who were delighted with them, and promised to come the next day, to buy and carry away any amount of them. She began to grow more cheerful, though she felt no appetite, and instead of eating everything, as she always did at picnics, she could not even touch Mattie Somers's cream pie nor Julia Dale's doughnuts. She stayed as late as she could at her friend Mattie's, but she felt she must get home in time for her third wish, at twelve o'clock.

Would it be necessary for her to wish that Ben Sykes' neck should be made shorter? She hoped it had grown shorter in the night, then she could do as she pleased about her third wish.

She still clung to the desire for the chariot and four. If she had it, she and her mother and Jimmy could get into it and drive far away from everybody – from Ben Sykes and his long neck, if he still had it – and never see any of them anymore. Still, she would like to show the chariot and four to her friends, and perhaps Ben Sykes would not mind

his long neck, and would be glad to keep it and earn money by showing himself at a circus.

So she reached home in the middle of the morning, and found the whole Sykes family there, and Ben, still with his long neck. It seems it had given him great trouble in the night. He had to sleep with his head in the opposite house, because there was not room enough on one floor at home. Mrs Sykes had not slept a wink, and her husband had been up watching, to see that nobody stepped on Ben's neck. Ben himself appeared in good spirits, but was glad to sit in a high room, where he could support his head.

They were all in the parlour, where the chocolate creams were partially cleared away. They were in a row on two sides of the room, meeting near the centre, with the underground passage, through which Ben had worked his way to Carrie's dress. Mrs Fraser had organized a band to fill pasteboard boxes, which she had obtained from the village, and she and her friends were filling them, to send away to be sold. All the inhabitants of the town were fed up with chocolate creams.

At this moment Carrie heard a click in the clock. She looked at her mother, and as the clock struck she said steadily, "I wish that Ben's neck was all right again."

Nobody heard her, for at that moment Ben Sykes started up, saying, "I'm all right, and I have had enough. Come along home!" And he dragged his family away with him.

Carrie fell into her mother's arms. "I'll never say 'chock full' again!" she cried, "and I'll always be satisfied with what I have got, for I can never forget what I suffered in seeing Ben's long neck!"

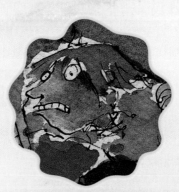

Lazy Jack

By Flora Annie Steel

Once upon a time there was a boy whose name was Jack, and he lived with his mother on a common. They were very poor, and the old woman got her living by spinning, but Jack was so lazy that he would do nothing but bask in the sun in the hot weather, and sit by the corner of the hearth in winter time. So they called him Lazy Jack. His mother could not get him to do anything for her, and at last told him, one Monday, that if he did not begin to work for his porridge she would turn him out to get his living as he could.

This roused Jack, and he went out and hired himself for the next day to a neighbouring farmer for a penny, but as he was coming home, never having had any money before, he lost it in passing over a brook.

"You stupid boy," said his mother, "you should have put it in your pocket."

"I'll do so another time," replied Jack.

Well, the next day, Jack went out again and hired himself to a cowkeeper, who gave him a jar of milk for his day's work. Jack took the jar and put it into the large pocket of his jacket, spilling it all, long before he got home.

"Dear me!" said the old woman. "You should have carried it on your head."

"I'll do so another time," said Jack.

So the following day, Jack hired himself again to a farmer, who agreed to give him a cream cheese for his services. In the evening Jack took the cheese,

and went home with it on his head. By the time he got home the cheese was all spoilt, part of it being lost, and part matted with his hair.

"You stupid lout," said his mother, "you should have carried it very carefully in your hands."

"I'll do so another time," replied Jack.

Now the next day, Lazy Jack again went out, and hired himself to a baker, who would give him nothing for his work but a large tom-cat. Jack took the cat, and began carrying it very carefully in his hands, but in a short time pussy scratched him so much that he was compelled to let it go.

When he got home, his mother said to him, "You silly fellow, you should have tied it with a string, and dragged it along after you."

"I'll do so another time," said Jack.

So on the following day, Jack hired himself to a butcher, who rewarded him by the present of a shoulder of mutton. Jack took the mutton, tied it with a string, and trailed it along after him in the dirt, so that by the time he had got home the meat was spoilt. His mother was this time quite out of patience with him, for the next day was Sunday, and she was obliged to do with cabbage for her dinner.

"You ninney-hammer," said she to her son, "you should have carried it on your shoulder."

"I'll do so another time," replied Jack.

Well, on the Monday, Lazy Jack went once more and hired himself to a cattle-keeper, who gave him a donkey for his trouble. Now though Jack was strong he found it hard to hoist the donkey on his shoulders, but at last he did it, and began walking home slowly with his prize. Now it so happened that in the course of his journey he passed a house where a rich man lived with his only daughter, a beautiful girl, who was deaf and dumb. She had never laughed in her life, and the doctors said she would never speak till somebody made her laugh. So the father had given out that any man who made her laugh would receive her hand in marriage. Now

Lazy Jack

this young lady happened to be looking out of the window when Jack was passing by with the donkey on his shoulders, and the poor beast with its legs sticking up in the air was kicking violently and heehawing with all its might. The sight was so comical that she burst out laughing, and immediately recovered her speech and hearing. Her father was overjoyed, and fulfilled his promise by marrying her to Lazy Jack, who was thus made a rich gentleman. They lived in a large house, and Jack's mother lived with them in great happiness until she died.

The Three Sillies

By Joseph Jacobs

*O*nce upon a time there was a farmer and his wife who had one daughter, and she was courted by a gentleman. Every evening he used to come and see her, and stop to supper at the farmhouse, and the daughter used to be sent down into the cellar to draw the beer for supper. So one evening she had gone down to draw the beer, and she happened to look up at the ceiling while she was drawing, and she saw a mallet stuck in one of the beams. It must have been there a long, long time, but somehow or other she had never noticed it before, and she began thinking. She thought it was very dangerous to have that mallet there, and said to herself: "Suppose him and me was to be married, and we was to have a son, and he was to grow up to be a man, and come down into the cellar to draw the beer, like as I'm doing now, and the mallet was to fall on his head and kill him, what a dreadful thing it would be!" And she put down the candle and the jug, and sat herself down and began crying.

Well, they began to wonder upstairs how it was that she was so long drawing the beer, and her mother went down to see after her, and she found her sitting on the settle crying, and the beer running over the floor. "Why, whatever is the matter?" said her mother.

"Oh, mother!" said she, "look at that horrid mallet! Suppose we was to be married, and was to have a son, and he was to grow up, and was to come down to the cellar to draw the beer, and the mallet

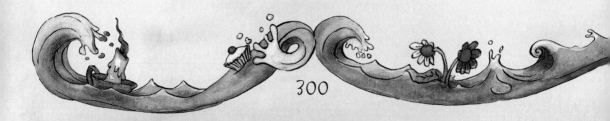

was to fall on his head and kill him, what a dreadful thing it would be!"

"Dear, dear! What a dreadful thing it would be!" said the mother, and she sat her down aside of the daughter and started crying too. Then after a bit the father began to wonder that they didn't come back, and he went down into the cellar to look after them himself, and there they two sat crying, and the beer running all over the floor. "Whatever is the matter?" said he.

"Why," said the mother, "look at that horrid mallet. Just suppose, if our daughter and her sweetheart was to be married, and was to have a son, and he was to grow up, and was to come down into the cellar to draw the beer, and the mallet was to fall on his head and kill him, what a dreadful thing it would be!"

"So it would!" said the father, and he sat himself down aside of the other two, and started crying.

Now the gentleman got tired of stopping up in

the kitchen by himself, and at last he went down into the cellar too, to see what they were after, and there they three sat crying side by side, and the beer running all over the floor. And he ran straight and turned the tap. Then he said: "Whatever are you three doing, sitting there crying, and letting the beer run all over the floor?"

"Oh!" said the father, "look at that horrid mallet! Suppose you and our daughter was to be married, and was to have a son, and he was to grow up, and was to come down into the cellar to draw the beer, and the mallet was to fall on his head and kill him!"

And then they all started crying worse than before. But the gentleman burst out laughing, and reached up and pulled out the mallet. Then he said: "I've travelled many miles, and I never met three such big sillies as you three. I shall set out on my travels again, and when I can find three bigger sillies than you three, I'll come back and marry your daughter." He wished them goodbye, and left them

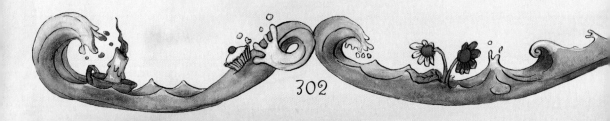

all crying because the girl had lost her sweetheart.

Well, he set out, and he travelled a long way, and at last he came to a woman's cottage that had some grass growing on the roof. And the woman was trying to get her cow to go up a ladder to the grass, and it would not go. So the gentleman asked the woman what she was doing. "Why," she said, "look at all that beautiful grass. I'm going to get the cow on to the roof to eat it. She'll be safe, for I shall tie a string round her neck, and pass it down the chimney, and tie it to my wrist as I go about the house, so she can't fall off without my knowing."

"Oh, you poor silly!" said the gentleman. "You should cut the grass and throw it down to the cow!" But the woman thought it was easier to get the cow up the ladder than to get the grass down, so she pushed and coaxed her up, and tied a string round her neck, and passed it down the chimney, and fastened it to her wrist.

The gentleman went on his way, but he hadn't

gone far when the cow tumbled off the roof, and hung by the string tied round its neck. The weight of the cow tied to her wrist pulled the woman up the chimney, and she stuck fast halfway and was covered in soot. Well, that was one big silly.

The gentleman travelled on, stopping at an inn for the night. As they were so full, the inn had to put him in a double-bedded room, and another traveller was to sleep in the other bed. The other man was a pleasant fellow, but in the morning, the gentleman was surprised to see the other hang his trousers on the knobs of the chest of drawers and run across the room and try to jump into them. He tried over and over again, and couldn't manage it, and the gentleman wondered whatever he was doing it for.

At last he stopped and wiped his face with his handkerchief. "Oh dear," he said, "I do think trousers are the most awkward kind of clothes that ever were. I can't think who could have invented such things. It takes me the best part of an hour to get into mine every morning, and I get so hot! How do you manage yours?"

So the gentleman burst out laughing, and showed him how to put them on, and he was very much obliged to him, and said he never should have thought of doing it that way. So that was another big silly.

The gentleman went on his travels again, and he came to a village. There was a pond with a crowd of people around it. And they had rakes and brooms and pitchforks reaching into the pond. The gentleman asked what was the matter.

The Three Sillies

"Why," they said, "the moon's tumbled into the pond, and we can't rake her out!" The gentleman began laughing, and told them that it was only the shadow in the water. But they wouldn't listen to him, so he got away as quick as he could.

The gentleman realised there was a whole lot of sillies bigger than those three sillies at home. So he went home and married the farmer's daughter, and if they didn't live happy forever after, that's nothing to do with you or me.

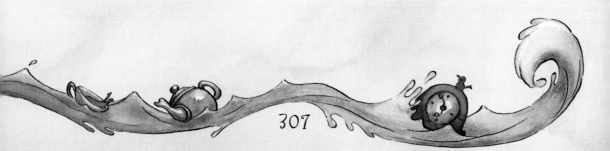

Tikki Tikki Tembo

Anon

*O*nce upon a time in faraway China there lived
two brothers, one named Sam, and one
named Tikki Tikki Tembo No Sarimbo Hari Kari
Bushkie Perry Pem Do Hai Kai Pom Pom Nikki No
Meeno Dom Barako.

Now one day the two brothers were playing near
the well in their garden when Sam fell into the well,
and Tikki Tikki Tembo No Sarimbo Hari Kari
Bushkie Perry Pem Do Hai Kai Pom Pom Nikki No
Meeno Dom Barako ran to his mother, shouting,

"Quick, Sam has fallen into the well!"

"What?" cried the mother, "Sam has fallen into the well? Run and tell father!"

Together they ran to the father and cried, "Quick, Sam has fallen into the well!"

"Sam has fallen into the well?" cried the father. "Run and tell the gardener!"

Then they all ran to the gardener and shouted, "Quick, Sam has fallen into the well."

"Sam has fallen into the well?" cried the gardener, and then he quickly fetched a ladder and pulled the poor boy from the well, who was wet and cold and frightened, and ever so happy to still be alive and well.

Some time afterward the

two brothers were again playing near the well. This
time Tikki Tikki Tembo No Sarimbo Hari Kari
Bushkie Perry Pem Do Hai Kai Pom Pom Nikki No
Meeno Dom Barako fell into the well, and Sam ran
to his mother, shouting, "Quick, Tikki Tikki
Tembo No Sarimbo Hari Kari Bushkie Perry Pem
Do Hai Kai Pom Pom Nikki No Meeno Dom
Barako has fallen into the well. What shall we do?"

"What?" cried the mother, "Tikki Tikki Tembo
No Sarimbo Hari Kari Bushkie Perry Pem Do Hai
Kai Pom Pom Nikki No Meeno Dom Barako has
fallen into the well? Run and tell father!"

Together they ran to the father and cried,
"Quick, Tikki Tikki Tembo No Sarimbo Hari Kari
Bushkie Perry Pem Do Hai Kai Pom Pom Nikki No
Meeno Dom Barako has fallen into the well. What
shall we do?"

"Tikki Tikki Tembo No Sarimbo Hari Kari
Bushkie Perry Pem Do Hai Kai Pom Pom Nikki No
Meeno Dom Barako has fallen into the well?" cried

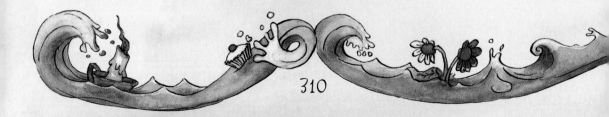

the father. "Run and tell the gardener!"

So they all ran to the gardener and shouted, "Quick, Tikki Tikki Tembo No Sarimbo Hari Kari Bushkie Perry Pem Do Hai Kai Pom Pom Nikki No Meeno Dom Barako has fallen into the well. What shall we do?"

"Tikki Tikki Tembo No Sarimbo Hari Kari Bushkie Perry Pem Do Hai Kai Pom Pom Nikki No Meeno Dom Barako has fallen into the well?" cried the gardener, and then he quickly fetched a ladder and pulled Tikki Tikki Tembo No Sarimbo Hari Kari Bushkie Perry Pem Do Hai Kai Pom Pom Nikki No Meeno Dom Barako from the well, but the poor boy had drowned.

And from that time forth, the Chinese have given their children short names.

BIRDS, BEASTS AND DRAGONS

My Lord
Bag of Rice

By Yei Theodora Ozaki

*L*ong, long ago there lived in Japan a brave
warrior known to all as Tawara Toda, or 'My
Lord Bag of Rice'. His true name was Fujiwara
Hidesato, and there is a very interesting story of
how he came to change his name.

One day he went out in search of adventures, for
he had the nature of a warrior and could not bear to
be idle. So he buckled on his two swords, took his

huge bow in his hand, and slinging his quiver on his back started out. He had not gone far when he came to the bridge of Seta-no-Karashi spanning one end of the beautiful Lake Biwa. No sooner had he set foot on the bridge than he saw lying right across his path a huge serpent-dragon. Its body was so big that it looked like the trunk of a large pine tree and it took up the whole width of the bridge. One of its huge claws rested on the parapet of one side of the bridge, while its tail lay right against the other. The monster seemed to be asleep, and as it breathed, fire and smoke came out of its nostrils.

At first Hidesato could not help feeling alarmed at the sight of this horrible reptile lying in his path, for he must either turn back or walk right over its body. He was a brave man, however, and putting aside all fear went forward dauntlessly. Crunch, crunch! He stepped now on the dragon's body, now between its coils, and without even one glance backward he went on his way.

He had only gone a few steps when he heard someone calling him from behind. On turning back he was much surprised to see that the monster dragon had entirely disappeared and in its place was a strange looking man, who was bowing most ceremoniously to the ground. His red hair streamed over his shoulders and was surmounted by a crown in the shape of a dragon's head, and his sea-green dress was patterned with shells. Hidesato knew at once that this was no ordinary mortal and he wondered much at the strange occurrence. Where had the dragon gone in such a short space of time? Or had it transformed itself into this man, and what did the whole thing mean? While

these thoughts passed through his mind he had
come up to the man on the bridge and now
addressed him:

"Was it you that called me just now?"

"Yes, it was I," said the man, "I have an earnest
request to make to you. Do you think you can grant
it to me?"

"If it is in my power to do so I will," answered
Hidesato, "but first tell me who you are."

"I am the dragon king of the lake, and my home
is in these waters just under this bridge."

"What is it you have to ask of me?" said
Hidesato.

"I want you to kill my mortal enemy the
centipede, who lives on the mountain beyond," and
the dragon king pointed to a high peak on the
opposite shore of the lake.

"I have lived for many years in this lake and I
have a large family of children and grandchildren.
For some time past we have lived in terror, for a

monster centipede has discovered our home, and night after night it comes and carries off one of my family. I am powerless to save them. If it goes on much longer like this, not only shall I lose all my children, but I myself must fall a victim to the monster. I am, therefore, very unhappy, and in my extremity I determined to ask the help of a human being. For many days with this intention I have waited on the bridge in the shape of the horrible serpent-dragon that you saw, in the hope that some strong brave man would come along. But all who came this way, as soon as they saw me were terrified and ran away as fast as they could. You are the first man I have found able to look at me without fear, so I knew at once that you were a man of great courage. I beg you to have pity upon me. Will you not help me and kill my enemy the centipede?"

Hidesato felt very sorry for the dragon king on hearing his story, and readily promised to do what he could to help him. The warrior asked where the

centipede lived, so that he might attack the creature at once. The dragon king replied that its home was on the mountain Mikami, but as it came every night at a certain hour to the palace of the lake, it would be better to wait till then.

So Hidesato was conducted to the palace of the dragon king, under the bridge. As he followed his host downwards the waters parted to let them pass. Amazingly his clothes did not even feel damp as he passed through the flood. Never had Hidesato seen anything so beautiful as this palace built of white marble beneath the lake. He had often heard of the sea king's palace at the bottom of the sea, where all the servants were saltwater fish, but here was a magnificent building in the heart of Lake Biwa. The dainty goldfish, red carp, and silvery trout, waited upon the dragon king and his guest.

Hidesato was astonished at the feast that was spread for him. The dishes were crystallized lotus leaves and flowers, and the chopsticks were of the

rarest ebony. As soon as they sat
down, the sliding doors
opened and ten lovely
goldfish dancers came out,
and behind them
followed ten red carp
musicians. Thus the hours flew
by till midnight, and
the beautiful music
and dancing had banished
all thoughts of the centipede. The
dragon king was about to pass the
warrior a cup of wine when the palace
was shaken by a tramp, tramp, tramp! It was
as if a mighty army had begun to march not far
away. Hidesato and his host both rose to their
feet and rushed to the balcony, and the warrior
saw on the opposite mountain two great balls of
glowing fire coming nearer and nearer. The dragon
king stood by the warrior's side trembling with fear.

"The centipede! Those two balls of fire are its eyes. It is coming for its prey! You must kill it."

Hidesato looked where his host pointed, and, in the dim light of the starlit evening, behind the two balls of fire he saw the long body of an enormous centipede winding round the mountains, and the light in its terrifying eyes glowed like many distant lanterns moving slowly towards the shore.

Hidesato showed no fear. He tried to calm the dragon king.

"Don't be afraid. I shall surely kill the centipede. Just bring me my bow and arrows."

The dragon king did as he was bid, and the warrior noticed that he had only three arrows left in his quiver. He took the bow, and fitting an arrow to the notch, took aim and let fly.

The arrow hit the centipede right in the middle of its head, but instead of penetrating, it glanced off harmless and fell to the ground.

Not daunted, Hidesato took another arrow, fitted it to the notch of the bow and let fly. Again the arrow hit the mark – it struck the centipede right in the middle of its head, only to glance off and fall to the ground. The centipede was invulnerable to weapons! When the dragon king saw that even this brave warrior's arrows were powerless to kill the centipede, he lost heart and began to tremble with fear.

The warrior saw that he had now only one arrow left in his quiver, and if this one failed he could not kill the centipede. He looked across the waters. The huge reptile had wound its horrid body seven times round the mountain and would soon come down to the lake. Nearer and nearer gleamed the fiery eyes, and the light of its hundred feet began to throw reflections in the still waters of the lake.

Then suddenly the warrior remembered
something! Human saliva was deadly to centipedes.
But this was no ordinary centipede. This was so
monstrous that even to think of such a creature
made him creep with horror. But Hidesato
determined to try one more time. So taking his last
arrow and first putting the end of it in his mouth,
he fitted the notch to his bow, took careful aim
once more and let his arrow fly.

The arrow again hit the centipede right in the
middle of its head, but instead of glancing off
harmlessly as before, it struck home to the creature's
brain. Then with a convulsive shudder the
serpentine body stopped moving, and the fiery light
of its great eyes and hundred feet darkened to a dull
glare like the sunset of a stormy day, and then went
out in blackness.

A great darkness now overspread the heavens,
thunder rolled and lightning flashed, and the wind
roared in fury, and it seemed as if the world were

coming to an end. The dragon king and his children and retainers all crouched in different parts of the palace, frightened to death, for the building was shaken to its foundation. At last the dreadful night was over. Day dawned beautiful and clear. The centipede was gone from the mountain.

Then Hidesato called to the dragon king to come out with him on the balcony, for the centipede was dead and he had nothing more to fear.

All the inhabitants of the palace came out shouting with joy, and Hidesato pointed to the lake. There lay the body of the dead centipede floating on the water, which was dyed red with its blood.

The gratitude of the dragon king knew no bounds. The whole family came and bowed down before the warrior, calling him their preserver and the bravest warrior in all Japan.

Another feast was prepared, more sumptuous than the first. All kinds of fish, prepared in every imaginable way, raw, stewed, boiled and roasted,

served on coral trays and crystal dishes, were put before him, and the wine was the best that Hidesato had ever tasted in his life. The sun shone brightly and the lake glittered like a liquid diamond. The palace was a thousand times more beautiful by day than by night.

His host tried to persuade the warrior to stay a few days, but Hidesato insisted on going home, saying that he had now finished what he had come to do, and must return.

The dragon king and his family were all very sorry to have him leave so soon, but since he would go they begged him to accept a few small presents (so they said) in token of their gratitude to him for delivering them forever from their terrible enemy the centipede.

As the warrior stood in the porch taking leave, a train of fish was suddenly transformed into a retinue of men, all wearing ceremonial robes and dragon's crowns on their heads to show that they

were servants of the great
dragon king. The presents
that they carried were as
follows:

First, a bronze bell.
Second, a bag of rice.
Third, a roll of silk.
Fourth, a cooking pot.
Fifth, another bell.

Hidesato did not want to accept all these
presents, but as the dragon king insisted, he could
not well refuse.

The dragon king himself accompanied the
warrior as far as the bridge, and then took leave of
him with many bows and good wishes, leaving the
procession of servants to accompany Hidesato to
his house with the presents.

The warrior's household and servants had been

very much concerned when they found that he did not return the night before, but they finally concluded that he had been kept by the violent storm and had taken shelter somewhere. When the servants on the watch for his return caught sight of him they called to everyone that he was approaching, and the whole household turned out to meet him, wondering what the retinue of men, bearing presents and banners, that followed him, could mean.

As soon as the dragon king's retainers had put down the presents they vanished, and Hidesato told all that had happened to him.

The presents that he had received from the grateful dragon king were found to be of magic power. Only the bell was ordinary, and as Hidesato had no use for it he presented it to the temple nearby, where it was hung up, to boom out the hour of day over the neighbourhood.

However much was taken from the single bag of

rice for the meals of the warrior and his whole family, the supply in the bag never grew less.

The roll of silk, too, never grew shorter, though time after time long pieces were cut off to make the warrior a new suit of clothes to go to court in at the New Year.

The cooking pot was magical, too. No matter what was put into it, it cooked deliciously whatever was wanted without any heating – truly a very economical saucepan.

The fame of Hidesato's fortune spread far and wide, and as there was no need for him to spend money on rice, silk or heating, he became very rich and prosperous, and was henceforth known as 'My Lord Bag of Rice'.

The Girl who Owned a Bear

By L Frank Baum

Mamma had gone downtown to shop. She had asked Nora to look after Jane Gladys, and Nora promised she would. But it was her afternoon for polishing the silver, so she stayed in the pantry and left Jane Gladys to amuse herself alone in the big sitting room upstairs. The little girl did not mind being alone, for she was working on her first piece of embroidery – a sofa pillow for papa's birthday present. So she crept into the big bay window and curled herself up on the broad windowsill while she bent her head over her work.

Soon the door opened and closed again, quietly. Jane Gladys thought it was Nora, so she didn't look up until she had taken a couple more stitches on a forget-me-not. Then she raised her eyes and was astonished to find a strange man in the middle of the room, who regarded her earnestly.

He was short and fat, and seemed to be breathing heavily from his climb up the stairs. He held a hat in one hand and underneath his other elbow was tucked a good-sized book. He was dressed in a black suit that looked old and rather shabby, and his head was bald upon the top.

"Excuse me," he said, while the child gazed at him in surprise. "Are you Jane Gladys Brown?"

"Yes, sir," she answered.

"Very good, very good, indeed!" he remarked, with a queer sort of smile. "I've had quite a hunt to

330

find you, but I've succeeded at last."

"How did you get in?" inquired Jane Gladys, with a growing distrust of her visitor.

"That is a secret," he said, mysteriously.

This was enough to put the girl on her guard. She looked at the man and the man looked at her, and both looks were grave and somewhat anxious.

"What do you want?" she asked, straightening herself up with a dignified air.

"Ah! Now we are coming to business," said the man, briskly. "I'm going to be quite frank with you, girl. Your father has abused me in a most ungentlemanly manner."

Jane Gladys got off the windowsill and pointed her small finger at the door.

"Leave this room 'meejitly!" she cried, her voice trembling with indignation. "My papa is the best man in the world. He never abused anybody!"

"Allow me to explain, please," said the visitor, without paying any attention to her request to go away. "Your father may be very kind to you, for you are his little girl. But when he's in his office he's inclined to be rather severe, especially on book agents. I called on him the other day and asked him to buy the 'Complete Works of Peter Smith,' and what do you suppose he did? He ordered me from his office, and had me put out of the building by the janitor! What do you think of such treatment as that from the 'best papa in the world,' eh?"

"I think he was quite right," said Jane Gladys.

"Oh, you do? Well," said the man, "I resolved to be revenged. So, as your father is big and strong I have decided to be revenged upon his little girl."

"What are you going to do?" she asked.

"I'm going to present you with this book," he answered, taking it from under his arm. Then he sat down on the edge of a chair, placed his hat on the rug and drew a fountain pen from his vest pocket.

"I'll write your name in it," said he. "How do you spell Gladys?"

"G-l-a-d-y-s," she replied.

"Thank you. Now this," he continued, rising and handing her the book with a bow, "is my revenge for your father's treatment of me. Perhaps he'll be sorry he didn't buy the 'Complete Works of Peter Smith.' Goodbye, my dear."

He walked to the door, gave her another bow, and left the room, and Jane Gladys could see that he was laughing to himself as if very much amused.

When the door had closed behind the strange little man the child sat down in the window again and glanced at the book. It had a red and yellow cover and the word 'Thingamajigs' was written across the front cover in big letters.

Then she opened it, curiously, and saw her name written in black letters upon the first white page.

"He was a funny little man," she said to herself, thoughtfully.

She turned the next page, and saw a big picture of a clown, dressed in green and red and yellow. He

334

had a very white face with three-cornered spots of red on each cheek and over the eyes. While she looked at this the book trembled in her hands, the page crackled and creaked, and suddenly the clown jumped out of it and stood upon the floor beside her, becoming instantly as big as a normal clown.

After stretching his arms and legs and yawning in a rather impolite manner, he gave a silly chuckle and said, "This is better! You don't know how cramped one gets, standing so long upon a page of flat paper."

Perhaps you can imagine how startled Jane Gladys was, and how she stared at the clown who had just leapt out of the book.

"You didn't expect anything of this sort, did you?" he asked, leering at her in clown fashion. Then he turned around to take a look at the room and Jane Gladys laughed in spite of her astonishment.

"What amuses you?" demanded the clown.

"Why, the back of you is all white!" cried the

girl. "You're only a clown in front of you."

"Quite likely," he returned, in an annoyed tone. "The artist made a front view of me. He wasn't expected to make the back of me, for that was against the page of the book."

"But it makes you look so funny!" said Jane Gladys, laughing until her eyes filled with tears.

The clown looked sulky and sat down upon a chair so she couldn't see his back.

"I'm not the only thing in the book," he remarked, crossly.

This reminded her to turn another page, and she had scarcely noted that it contained the picture of a monkey when the animal sprang from the book with a great crumpling of paper and landed upon the window seat beside her.

"He he he he he!" chattered the creature, springing to the girl's shoulder and then to the centre table. "This is great fun! Now I can be a real monkey instead of a picture of one."

"Real monkeys can't talk," said Jane Gladys.

"How do you know? Have you ever been one yourself?" inquired the animal, and then he laughed loudly.

The girl was quite bewildered by this time. She turned another page, and before she had time to look twice a grey donkey leapt from the book and stumbled from the window seat to the floor with a great clatter.

"You're clumsy enough, I'm sure!" said the child, indignantly, for the beast had nearly upset her.

"Clumsy! And why not?" demanded the donkey, in an angry voice. "If the silly artist had drawn you out of perspective, as he did me, I guess you'd be clumsy yourself."

"What's wrong with you?" asked Jane Gladys.

"My front and rear legs on the left side are nearly six inches too short, that's what's the matter! If that artist didn't know how to draw properly why did he try to make a donkey at all?"

"I don't know," replied the child.

"I can hardly stand up," grumbled the donkey, "and the least little thing will topple me over."

"Don't mind that," said the monkey, making a spring at the chandelier and swinging from it by his tail until Jane Gladys feared he would knock all the globes off. "The artist has made my ears as big as that clown's, and everyone knows a monkey hasn't any ears to speak of – much less to draw."

"He should be prosecuted," remarked the clown, gloomily. "I haven't any back."

Jane Gladys looked from one to the other with a puzzled expression upon her sweet face, and turned another page of the book.

Swift as a flash there sprang over her shoulder a tawny, spotted leopard, which landed upon the back of a big leather armchair and turned upon the others with a fierce movement.

The monkey climbed to the top of the chandelier and chattered with fright. The donkey tried to run but straightway tipped over onto his left side. The clown grew paler than ever, but he sat still in his chair and gave a low whistle of surprise.

The leopard crouched upon the back of the chair, lashed his tail from side to side and glared at all of them, by turns, including Jane Gladys.

"Which of us are you going to attack first?" asked the donkey.

"I can't attack any of you," snarled the leopard. "The artist made my mouth shut, so I haven't any teeth, and he forgot to make my claws. But I'm a frightful looking creature, nevertheless, am I not?"

"Oh, yes," said the clown. "I suppose you are frightful-looking enough. But if you have no teeth nor claws we don't mind your looks at all."

This annoyed the leopard so much that he growled horribly, and the monkey laughed at him.

Just then the book slipped from the girl's lap, and

as she went to catch it one of the pages near the
back opened wide. She saw a grizzly bear looking at
her from the page, and threw the book to the
ground. It fell in the middle of the
room, and beside it stood the great
grizzly, who had wrenched himself
from the page
before the book
had closed.

"Now," cried the leopard from his perch, "you'd better look out for yourselves! You can't laugh at him as you did at me. For the bear has both claws and teeth."

"Indeed I have," said the bear, in a low, deep, growling voice. "And I know exactly how to use them, too. If you read in that book you'll find I'm described as a remorseless, vicious grizzly bear, whose only business in life is to eat up little girls – shoes, dresses, ribbons and all! And then, the author says, I smack my lips and glory in my wickedness."

"That's absolutely awful!" said the donkey, sitting upon his haunches and shaking his head sadly at this news. "What do you suppose possessed the author to make you so hungry for girls? Do you eat animals, too?"

"The author does not mention my eating anything at all but little girls, and so that is what I must do," replied the bear.

"Very good," remarked the clown, drawing a long breath of relief. "You may begin eating Jane Gladys as soon as you would like, because she laughed at me for having no back."

"And she laughed because my legs are out of perspective," brayed the donkey.

"But you also deserve to be eaten," shouted the leopard, loudly, from the back of the leather chair, "for you laughed and poked fun at me because I had no claws nor teeth! Don't you suppose Mr Grizzly, you could manage to eat a clown, a donkey and a monkey after you finish the girl?"

"Perhaps so, and a leopard into the bargain," growled the bear. "It will depend on how hungry I am. But I must begin on the little girl first, because the author says I prefer girls to anything, and I must do as the author wrote."

Jane Gladys was much frightened on hearing this conversation, and she began to realize what the man meant when he said he gave her the book to be

revenged. After all, surely papa would be ever so sorry he hadn't bought the 'Complete Works of Peter Smith' when he came home and found his little girl eaten up by a grizzly bear – shoes, dress, ribbons and all!

The bear stood up and balanced himself on his rear legs.

"This is the way I look in the book," he said. "Now watch me eat the little girl."

He advanced slowly towards Jane Gladys, and the monkey, the leopard, the donkey and the clown all stood around in a circle and watched the bear with much interest. But before the grizzly bear reached her the child had a sudden brilliant thought, and cried out, "Stop! You mustn't eat me. It would be wrong."

"Why?" asked the bear, in surprise.

"Because I own you. You're my private property," she answered.

"I don't see how you make that out," said the

grizzly bear, in a disappointed tone.

"Why, the book was given to me, Jane Gladys Brown. My name is on the front page after all. And you belong, by rights, in the book. So you must not dare to eat your owner!"

The grizzly bear hesitated.

"Can any of you read?" he asked.

"I can," said the clown.

"Then see if she speaks the truth. Is her name really written in the book?"

The clown picked it up and looked at the name.

"It is," said he. "Jane Gladys Brown, and written quite plainly in big letters."

The bear gave a loud sigh.

"Then, of course, I can't eat her," he decided. "That author is ever so disappointing – as most authors are."

"But he's not as bad as the artist," exclaimed the donkey, who was still trying to stand up straight, without any success.

"The fault lies with yourselves," said Jane Gladys, severely. "Why didn't you stay in the book, where you were put?"

The animals looked at each other in a foolish way, and the clown blushed with embarrassment under his white paint.

"Really," began the bear, and then he stopped.

The doorbell rang loudly.

"It's mamma!" cried Jane Gladys, springing to her feet. "She's come home at last. Now, you stupid creatures—"

But she was interrupted by them all making a rush for the book. There was a swish and a whirr and a rustling of leaves, and an instant later the book lay upon the floor looking just like any other book, while Jane Gladys' strange companions had completely disappeared, and she was safe at last.

This story should teach us to think quickly and clearly upon all occasions, for had Jane Gladys not remembered that she owned the bear he probably would have eaten her before the bell rang.

The Two Frogs

By Andrew Lang

Once upon a time in Japan there lived two frogs, one of whom made his home in a ditch near the town of Osaka, on the sea coast, while the other dwelt in a clear little stream that ran through the city of Kyoto. At such a great distance apart, they had never even heard of each other, but, funnily enough, the idea came into both their heads at once that they should like to see a little of the world. The frog who lived at Kyoto wanted to visit Osaka, and the frog who lived at Osaka wished to go to Kyoto, where the great Mikado had his palace.

So one fine morning in the spring they both set out along the road that led from Kyoto to Osaka, one from one end and the other from the other. The journey was more tiring than they expected, for they did not know much about travelling, and halfway between the two towns there arose a mountain that had to be climbed. It took them a long time and a great many hops to reach the top, but there they were at last, and what was the surprise of each to see another frog before him!

They looked at each other for a moment without speaking, and then fell into conversation, explaining the cause of their meeting so far from their homes. It was delightful to find that they both felt the same wish – to learn a little more of their native country – and as there was no sort of hurry they stretched themselves out in a cool, damp place, and agreed that they would have a good rest before they parted to go their ways.

The Two Frogs

"What a pity we are not bigger," said the Osaka frog, "then we could see both towns from here, and tell if it is worth our while going on."

"Oh, that is easily managed," returned the Kyoto frog. "We have only got to stand up on our hind legs, and hold onto each other, and then we can each look at the town he is travelling to."

This idea pleased the Osaka frog so much that he at once jumped up and put his front feet on the shoulder of his friend, who had risen also. There they both stood, stretching themselves as high as they could, and holding each other tightly, so that they might not fall down. The Kyoto frog turned his nose towards Osaka, and the Osaka frog turned his nose towards

Kyoto. But the foolish things forgot that when they stood up their great eyes lay in the backs of their heads, and that though their noses might point to the places to which they wanted to go, their eyes beheld the places from which they had come.

"Dear me!" cried the Osaka frog, "Kyoto is exactly like Osaka. It is certainly not worth such a long journey. I shall go home!"

"If I had had any idea that Osaka was only a copy of Kyoto I should never have travelled all this way," exclaimed the frog from Kyoto. As he spoke he took his hands from his friend's shoulders and they both fell down on the grass. Then they took a polite farewell of each other and set off for home again. To the end of their lives they believed that Osaka and Kyoto, which are as different to look at as two towns can be, were as alike as two peas in a pod.

How the Rhinoceros got his Skin

By Rudyard Kipling

A Parsee is a member of a religious sect mainly found in India, although the religion started in Persia (modern day Iran). Nowadays, it is usually spelt 'Parsi'.

*O*nce upon a time, on an uninhabited island on the shores of the Red Sea, there lived a Parsee from whose hat the rays of the sun were reflected in oriental splendour. And the Parsee lived by the Red

Sea with nothing but his hat, knife and a cooking stove of the kind that you must never touch.

One day he took flour and water and currants and plums and sugar and things, and made himself one cake that was two feet across and three feet thick. It was indeed a superior dish, and he put it on the stove because he was allowed to cook on that stove, and he baked it and he baked it till it was all done brown and smelt most delicious. But just as he was going to eat it there came down to the beach from the Altogether Uninhabited Interior one rhinoceros with a horn on his nose, two piggy eyes and few manners. In those days the rhinoceros' skin fitted him quite tight. There were no wrinkles in it anywhere. He looked exactly like a Noah's ark rhinoceros, but of course much bigger. All the same, he had no manners then, and he has no manners now, and he never will have any manners.

He said, "How!" and the Parsee left that cake and climbed to the top of a palm tree with nothing on but his hat, from which the rays of the sun were always reflected in oriental splendour. And the rhinoceros upset the oil stove with his nose and the cake rolled on the sand, and he spiked that cake on the horn of his nose and he ate it, and he went away waving his tail, to the desolate and Exclusively Uninhabited Interior that is next to the islands of Mazanderan, Socotra and Promontories of the Larger Equinox. Then the Parsee came down from his palm tree and put the stove on its legs and recited the following poem, which, as you have not heard, I will now proceed to relate:

> "*Them that takes cakes*
> *Which the Parsee man bakes*
> *Makes dreadful mistakes.*"

And there was a great deal more in that than you would think. Because, five weeks later, there was a heatwave in the Red Sea, and everybody took off all the clothes they had on. The Parsee took off his hat but the Rhinoceros took off his skin and carried it over his shoulder as he came down to the beach to bathe. In those days it buttoned underneath with three buttons and looked like a waterproof. He said nothing whatever about the Parsee's cake, because he had eaten it all, and he never had any manners, then, since, or henceforward. He waddled straight into the water and blew bubbles through his nose, leaving his skin on the beach.

Presently the Parsee came by and found the skin, and he smiled one smile that ran all round his face two times. Then he danced three times round the skin and rubbed his hands. Then he went to his camp and filled his hat with cake crumbs, for the Parsee never ate anything but cake, and never swept out his camp. He took that skin, and he shook that skin, and he scrubbed that skin, and he rubbed that skin just as full of old, dry, stale, tickly cake crumbs and some burnt currants as ever it

could possibly hold. Then he climbed to the top of his palm tree and waited for the rhinoceros to come out of the water and put it on.

And the rhinoceros did. He buttoned it up with the three buttons, and it tickled like cake crumbs in bed. Then he wanted to scratch, but that made it worse, and then he lay down on the sands and rolled and rolled and rolled, and every time he rolled the cake crumbs tickled him worse and worse and worse. Then he ran to the palm tree and rubbed and rubbed and rubbed himself against it. He rubbed so much and so hard that he rubbed his skin into a great fold over his shoulders and another fold underneath, where the buttons used to be (but he rubbed the buttons off) and he rubbed some more folds over his legs. And it spoiled his temper, but it didn't make the least difference to the cake crumbs. They were inside his skin and they tickled. So he went home, very angry indeed and horribly scratchy, and from that day to this every rhinoceros has great folds in his skin and a very bad temper, all on account of the cake crumbs inside.

But the Parsee came down from his palm tree, wearing his hat, from which the rays of the sun were reflected in oriental splendour, packed up his cooking stove and went away in the direction of Orotavo, Amygdala, the Upland Meadows of Anantarivo and the Marshes of Sonaput.

The Seven Little Kids

By the Brothers Grimm

*T*here was once a mother goat who had seven little kids, and was as fond of them as every mother was of her children. One day she had to go into the wood to fetch food for them, so she called them all round her.

"Dear children," said she, "I am going out into the wood and while I am gone, be on your guard against the wolf, for if he were once to get inside he would eat you up, skin, bones and all. The wretch often disguises himself, but he may always be known by his hoarse voice and black paws."

"Mother," answered the kids, "you need not be afraid, we will take care of ourselves." And the mother bleated goodbye, and went on her way with an easy mind.

It was not long before someone came knocking at the door, and crying out, "Open the door, my dear children. Your mother has come back, and brought each of you something."

But the kids knew it was the wolf by the hoarse voice. "We will not open the door," they cried, "you are not our mother. She has a delicate voice, and your voice is hoarse – you must be the wolf!"

So the wolf went to a shop and bought a big lump of chalk, and ate it up to make his voice soft. Then he came back, knocked at the door and cried, "Open the door, my dear children. Your mother is here, and has brought each of you something."

The Seven Little Kids

But the wolf had put his black paws up against the window, and the kids seeing this, cried out, "We will not open the door, our mother has no black paws like you – you must be the wolf!"

The wolf then ran to a baker.

"Baker," said he, "I have hurt my feet, pray spread some dough over them."

And when the baker had plastered his feet with dough, the wolf ran to the miller.

"Miller," said he, "cover my paws with some white flour." But the miller refused, thinking the wolf must be meaning harm to someone.

"If you don't do it," cried the wolf, "I'll eat you!"

And the miller was afraid and did as he was told. And that just shows what men are.

Now the wolf arrived at the door for a third time and knocked. "Open, children!" cried he. "Your dear mother has come home, and brought you each something from the wood."

"First show us your paws," said the kids, "so that

we may know if you are really our mother or not."

The wolf put his paws against the window, and when the kids saw that they were white, all seemed right and safe, so they opened the door to let their mother in.

But when they opened the door and he came inside they saw it was the wolf after all, and the terrified kids tried to hide themselves around the house at once.

One ran under the table, the second got into the bed, the third into the oven, the fourth in the kitchen, the fifth in the cupboard, the sixth under the sink and the seventh in the clock-case. But the wolf searched and found them all.

One after the other, he quickly swallowed the kids down – all but the youngest, who was hidden in the clock-case. So the wolf, having got what he wanted at last, strolled forth into the green meadow outside, and laying himself down under a tree, fell into a deep sleep.

It was not long after, however, that the mother goat came back from the wood, and, oh! What a horrible sight met her eyes! The door was standing wide open. The table, chairs and stools were all thrown about. Dishes were broken, and the quilt and pillows were torn off the bed. She knew at once that the wolf had been.

She sought her children, but they were nowhere to be found. The mother goat called to each of them by name, hoping that they had managed to hide. Nobody answered until she came to the name of the youngest kid.

"Here I am, mother," a little voice cried, "here, in the clock-case."

And so she helped him out and heard what had happened. And you may think how she cried for the loss of her dear children. At last she wandered outdoors with her youngest kid, and when they got to the meadow, they saw the wolf sleeping under a tree. The mother goat noticed how the wolf's body was moving and struggling.

'Dear me!' thought she, 'can it be that my poor children are still alive?' And she sent the little kid back to the house for a pair of shears, and needle, and thread. She cut the wolf's body open and one by one the six little kids all jumped out alive. The wolf had swallowed them whole!

"Now fetch some stones," said the mother, "and we will fill his body with them."

And so they fetched some stones, put

them inside the wolf, and the mother sewed him up. When the wolf at last awoke, and got up, the stones inside him made him feel very thirsty. As he was going to the brook to drink, they struck and rattled one against another. And so he cried out:

"What is this I feel inside me
Knocking hard against my bones?
How should such a thing betide me!
They were kids, and now they're stones."

So he came to the brook and stooped to drink, but the heavy stones weighed him down, and he fell into the water and was drowned. And when the seven little kids saw it they came running up.

"The wolf is dead!" they cried, and they danced with their mother all about the place.

The Sagacious Monkey and the Boar

By Yei Theodora Ozaki

*L*ong, long ago, there lived in the province of Shinshin in Japan, a travelling monkey man, who earned his living by taking round a monkey and showing off the animal's tricks. One evening the man came home in a very bad temper and told his wife to send for the butcher the next morning.

His wife was very bewildered and asked her husband, "Why do you wish me to send for the butcher?"

"It's no use taking that monkey round any longer, he's too old and forgets his tricks. I beat him with my stick all I know how, but he won't dance properly. I must now sell him to the butcher and make what money out of him I can. There is nothing else to be done."

The woman felt very sorry for the poor little animal, and pleaded for her husband to spare the monkey, but her pleading was all in vain, the man was determined to sell him to the butcher.

Now the monkey was in the next room and overheard every word of the conversation. He soon understood that he was to be killed, and he said to himself, "Barbarous, indeed, is my master! Here I have served him faithfully for years, and instead of allowing me to end my days comfortably and in peace, he is going to let me be cut up by the butcher, and my poor body is to be roasted and stewed and eaten! Woe is me! What am I to do? Ah! A bright thought has struck me! There is a wild boar living in the forest nearby. I have often heard tell of his wisdom. Perhaps if I go to him and tell him the strait I am in he will give me his counsel. I will go and try."

There was no time to lose. The monkey slipped out of the house and ran as quickly as he could to the forest to find the boar. The boar was at home, and the monkey began his tale of woe at once. "Good Mr Boar, I have heard of your excellent wisdom. I am in great trouble. You alone can help me. I have grown old in the service of my master, and because I cannot dance properly now he intends to sell me to the butcher. What do you advise me to do? I know how clever you are!"

The boar was pleased at the flattery and determined to help the monkey. He thought for a while and then said, "Hasn't your master a baby?"

"Yes," said the monkey, "he has one infant son."

"Doesn't it lie by the door in the morning when your mistress begins the work of the day? I will come round early and when I see my opportunity I will seize the child and run off with it."

"What then?" said the monkey.

"Why the mother will be in a tremendous state, and before your master and mistress know what to do, you must run after me and rescue the child and take it home safely to its parents. You will see that when the butcher comes they won't have the heart to sell you."

The monkey thanked the boar many times and then went home. He did not sleep much that night, as you may imagine, for thinking of the next day. His life depended on whether the boar's plan succeeded or not. He was the first up, waiting anxiously for what was to happen. It seemed to him a long time before his master's wife began to move about and open the shutters to let in the light.

Luckily, everything happened as the boar had planned. The mother placed her child near the porch as usual while she tidied up the house and got her breakfast ready.

The child was crooning happily in the morning sunlight, dabbing on the mats at the play of light and shadow. Suddenly there was a noise in the porch and a loud cry from the child. The mother called her husband from the inner room where he was still sleeping soundly, and they both ran to the porch door just in time to see the boar disappearing with their child. Then they saw the monkey running after the thief as hard as his legs would carry him.

Both the man and wife were moved to admiration at the plucky conduct of the sagacious monkey, and their gratitude knew no bounds when the faithful monkey brought the child safely back to their arms.

"There!" said the wife. "This is the animal you want to kill – if the monkey hadn't been here we should have lost our child forever."

"You are right, wife," said the man as he carried the child into the house. "You may send the butcher back when he comes, and now give us all a good breakfast and the monkey too."

When the butcher arrived he was sent away with an order for some boar's meat for the evening dinner, and the monkey was petted and lived the rest of his days in peace, nor did his master ever strike him again.

How the Camel got his Hump

By Rudyard Kipling

*I*n the beginning of years, when the world was so new-and-all, and the animals were just beginning to work for man, there was a camel, and he lived in the middle of a howling desert because he did not want to work, and besides, he was a howler himself. So he ate sticks and thorns and tamarisks and milkweed and prickles. He was most frustratingly idle, and when anybody spoke to him he said

"Humph!" Just "Humph!" and no more.

Presently the horse came to him on Monday morning, with a saddle on his back and a bit in his mouth, and said, "Camel, come out and trot like the rest of us."

"Humph!" said the camel, and the horse went away and told the man.

Presently the dog came to him with a stick in his mouth, and said, "Camel, come and fetch and carry like the rest of us."

"Humph!" said the camel and the dog went away to tell the man.

Presently the ox came to him, with the yoke on his neck and said, "Camel, come and plough like the rest of us."

"Humph!" said the camel, and the ox went away and told the man.

At the end of the day the man called the horse and the dog and the ox together, and said, "Three, I'm very sorry for you (with the world so new-and-

all), but that humph-thing in the desert can't work, or he would have been here by now, so I am going to leave him alone. You must work double-time to make up for it."

That made the Three very angry (with the world

so new-and-all), and they held a palaver, and an indaba, and a punchayet, and a pow-wow on the edge of the desert, and the camel came chewing milkweed, and laughed at them. Then he said "Humph!" and went away again.

Presently there came along the djinn in charge of All Deserts, rolling in a cloud of dust (djinns always travel that way because it is magic), and he stopped to palaver and pow-wow with the Three.

"Djinn of All Deserts," said the horse, "is it right and proper for any one to be idle, with the world so new-and-all?"

"Certainly not," said the djinn.

"Well," said the horse, "there's a thing in the middle of your Howling Desert (and he's a howler himself) with a long neck and long legs, and he hasn't done a stroke of work since Monday morning. He won't trot."

"Whew!" said the djinn, whistling, "that's my camel. What does he say about it?"

How the Camel got his Hump

"He says Humph!" said the dog, "and he won't fetch and carry."

"Does he say anything else?"

"He only says 'Humph'. And he won't plough," said the ox.

"Very good," said the djinn. "I'll humph him if you will kindly wait a minute."

The djinn rolled himself up in his dust-cloak, and took a bearing across the desert. The djinn found the camel looking at his own reflection in a pool of water.

"My long and bubbling friend," said the djinn, "what's this I hear of you doing no work, with the world so new-and-all?"

"Humph!" said the camel.

The djinn sat down, with his chin in his hand, and began to think a great magic, while the camel looked at his own reflection in the pool of water.

"You've given the Three extra work ever since Monday morning, all on account of your idleness," said the djinn, and he went on thinking magics, with his chin in his hand.

"Humph!" said the camel.

"I shouldn't say that again if I were you," said the djinn, "you might say it once too often. I want you to work."

And the camel said "Humph!" again, but no sooner had he said it than he saw his back, that he was so proud of, puffing up and up into a great big lolloping humph.

"Do you see that?" said the djinn. "That's your own humph that you've brought upon your own self by not working. Today is Thursday, and you've

done no work since Monday, when the work began.
Now you are going to work."

"How can I," said the camel, "with this humph
on my back?"

"That's made on purpose," said the djinn, "all
because you missed those three days. You will be
able to work now for three days without eating,
because you can live on your humph. Don't you
ever say I never did anything for you. Come out of
the desert and go to the Three, and behave!"

And the camel humphed himself, humph and all,
and went away to join the Three. And from that day
to this the camel always wears a humph (we call it
'hump' now, not to hurt his feelings) but he has
never yet caught up with the three days that he
missed at the beginning of the world, and he has
never yet learned how to behave.

Why the Swallow's Tail is Forked

By Florence Holbrook

This is the story of how the swallow's tail came to be forked. One day the Great Spirit asked all the animals that he had made to come to his lodge. Those that could fly came first – the robin, the bluebird, the owl, the butterfly, the wasp and the firefly. Behind them came the chicken, fluttering its wings and trying hard to keep up. Then came the deer, the squirrel, the serpent, the

378

cat and the rabbit. Last of all came the bear, the beaver and the hedgehog. Every one travelled as swiftly as he could, for each wished to hear the words of the Great Spirit.

"I have called you together," said the Great Spirit, "because I often hear you scold and fret. What do you wish me to do for you? How can I help you?"

"I do not like to hunt so long for my food," said the bear.

"I do not like to build nests," said the bluebird.

"I do not like living in water," said the beaver.

"I do not like to live in a tree," said the squirrel.

At last man stood before the Great Spirit and said, "O Great Father, the serpent feasts upon my blood. Will you not give him some other food?"

"And why?" asked the Great Spirit.

"Because I am the first of all the creatures you have made," answered man proudly.

Every animal in the lodge was angry to hear the

words of man. The squirrel chattered, the wasp buzzed, the owl hooted and the serpent hissed.

"Hush, be still," said the Great Spirit. "You are, man, the first of my creatures, but I am the father of all. Each one has his rights, and the serpent must have his food. Mosquito, you are a great traveller. Now fly away and find what creature's blood is best for the serpent. You must all come back in a year and a day."

The animals straightway went to their homes. Some went to the river, some to the forest and some to the prairie, to wait for the day when they must meet at the lodge of the Great Spirit.

The mosquito travelled over the earth and stung every creature that he met to find whose blood was the best for the serpent. On his way back to the lodge of the Great Spirit he looked up into the sky and there was the swallow.

"Good day, swallow," called the mosquito.

"I am glad to see you, my friend," sang the

swallow. "Are you going to the lodge of the Great Spirit? Have you found out whose blood is best for the serpent?"

"The blood of man," answered the mosquito.

The mosquito did not like man, but the swallow had always been his friend. 'What can I do to help man?' he thought. 'Oh, I know what I can do.' Then he asked the mosquito, "Whose blood did you say?"

"Man's blood," said the mosquito, "that is best."

"This is best," said the swallow, and he tore out the mosquito's tongue.

The mosquito buzzed angrily and went quickly to the Great Spirit.

"All the animals are here," said the Great Spirit. "They are waiting to hear whose blood is best for the serpent."

The mosquito tried to answer, "The blood of man," but he could not say a word. He could make no sound but "Kss-ksss-ksssss!"

"What do you say?"

"Kss-ksss-ksssss!" buzzed the mosquito angrily.

All the creatures wondered. Then said the swallow, "Great Father, the mosquito is timid and cannot answer you. I met him before we came, and he told me whose blood it was."

"Let us know at once," said the Great Spirit.

"It is the blood of the frog," answered the swallow quickly. "Is it not so, friend mosquito?"

"Kss-ksss-ksssss!" hissed the angry mosquito.

"The serpent shall have the frog's blood," said the Great Spirit. "Man shall no longer be its food."

The serpent was angry with the swallow, for he did not like frog's blood. As the swallow flew near him, he seized him by the tail and tore away a little of it. This is why the swallow's tail is forked, and it is why man looks upon the swallow as his friend.

The End